THE LANDLADY'S MASTER

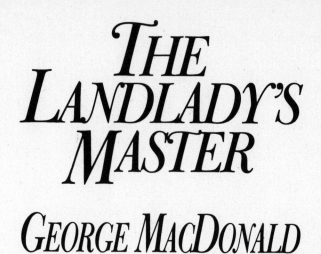

THE LANDLADY'S MASTER

GEORGE MACDONALD

BETHANY HOUSE PUBLISHERS
MINNEAPOLIS, MINNESOTA 55438
A Division of Bethany Fellowship, Inc.

Cover illustration by Dan Thornberg,
Bethany House Publishers staff artist.

Originally published in 1888 as *The Elect Lady*
by Kegan Paul, Trench, and Co., London.

Published by Bethany House Publishers
A Division of Bethany Fellowship, Inc.
6820 Auto Club Road, Minneapolis, Minnesota 55438

Printed in the United States of America

Library of Congress Cataloging-in-Publication Data

MacDonald, George, 1824–1905.
    The landlady's master / George MacDonald ; Michael R. Phillips, editor.
      p. cm.
    Rev. ed. of: The elect lady. c1888.
    I. Phillips, Michael R., 1946–   .
II. MacDonald, George, 1824–1905. Elect lady. III. Title.
    PR4967.E44   1989
823'.8—dc20   89–37344
ISBN 0-87123-904-3   CIP

BETHANY HOUSE PUBLISHERS
Minneapolis, Minnesota 55438

The Novels of George MacDonald Edited for Today's Reader

Edited Title	Original Title
The Fisherman's Lady	*Malcolm*
The Marquis' Secret	*The Marquis of Lossie*
The Baronet's Song	*Sir Gibbie*
The Shepherd's Castle	*Donal Grant*
The Tutor's First Love	*David Elginbrod*
The Musician's Quest	*Robert Falconer*
The Maiden's Bequest	*Alec Forbes*
The Curate's Awakening	*Thomas Wingfold*
The Lady's Confession	*Paul Faber*
The Baron's Apprenticeship	*There and Back*
The Highlander's Last Song	*What's Mine's Mine*
The Gentlewoman's Choice	*Weighed and Wanting*
The Laird's Inheritance	*Warlock O'Glenwarlock*
The Minister's Restoration	*Salted with Fire*
A Daughter's Devotion	*Mary Marston*
The Peasant Girl's Dream	*Heather and Snow*
The Landlady's Master	*The Elect Lady*
The Poet's Homecoming	*Home Again*

MacDonald Classics Edited for Young Readers

Wee Sir Gibbie of the Highlands
Alec Forbes and His Friend Annie
At the Back of the North Wind
The Adventures of Ranald Bannerman

———

George MacDonald: Scotland's Beloved Storyteller by Michael Phillips
Discovering the Character of God by George MacDonald
Knowing the Heart of God by George MacDonald
A Time to Grow by George MacDonald
A Time to Harvest by George MacDonald

Contents

8

Introduction

The Elect Lady, first published in 1888, stands out among George MacDonald's novels as shorter and less detailed in plot, characterization, and style. No doubt this apparent lack of depth explains why *The Elect Lady* is one of the least reprinted, least studied, and least widely known of MacDonald's books, with scant sales in the one hundred years since its release. I came to this project, therefore, with a bias probably shared by many familiar with MacDonald, of considering this title one of his less significant works. I am happy to say I was in for a delightful surprise! The book, as every MacDonald eventually does, took me over as I became more involved in it.

I am not going to claim that *The Elect Lady* ranks with MacDonald's greatest literary achievements, that it contains the stature of books like *Malcolm*, or *Sir Gibbie*. There is a simplicity to its style and a frustrating lack of development in the description and characterization that critics might point to as deficiencies. I found myself saying, "If only MacDonald had spent more time deepening these characters and expanding these themes!" Yet from another perspective, it hardly mattered.

I appreciate MacDonald's wonderful characters and their varied nuances of personality, emotion, and growth. I love his descriptions of the Scottish moors and mountains, seascapes and countryside. I relish his plot intricacies. But it is not *primarily* for his characters, his descriptive power, nor his plot-making ingenuity that I read MacDonald. What makes me savor his insights as a connoisseur might a fine wine, and brood over his words as a lover meditates upon the virtues of his beloved, is the God-breathed and, I firmly believe, supernatural wisdom he brings to bear upon my daily breathing, struggling, interactive, practical life with God—in the next five minutes, and all my life long.

That is George MacDonald's power: the capacity to open the heart hungry for greater revelations of truth, to deepen God's immediacy, to practicalize faith, to change attitudes and relationships by bringing God into every tiniest facet of them. Who is God, what is He like, how are we to relate ourselves to Him and obey Him and love Him, and how are our thought patterns and relationships and priorities to grow and change as a result? *These* are the questions to which George MacDonald gave his life as an author—not to mere descriptions and plots. His characters exist on the page to help me as a reader relate more intimately to God my maker, not to provide fodder for analysis. Whatever refinement may be missing on the literary side of *The Elect Lady* is found on the deeper spiritual level. The book offered wonderful insights that fed my soul.

MacDonald's perception on the subject of unity and the true composition and calling of God's church caused my greatest emotional response. There are those who take the comments of his characters and the author's own commentary in this book and others to conclude that MacDonald liked neither the church nor the pulpit and wanted nothing to do with either, pointing to MacDonald's repeated depiction of clergymen as shallow, insensitive misrepresentations of Christ.

I take the opposite view. Such portrayals reveal how deeply George MacDonald *did* love the church and how desperately he longed for it to emerge victorious into the fulfillment of its purpose. He criticized the system for the same reason God punishes sin—not to tear down and destroy, but to build up, redeem, and raise into righteousness. I look to some of MacDonald's shining saints—men like Sandy Graham, Harry Walton, Thomas Wingfold, the reformed James Blatherwick, the humble and growing Mr. Drake, and Robert Falconer's unnamed mentor whom he calls "one of the holy servants of God's great temple"—clergymen all—as evidences of just how greatly George MacDonald loved the clergy, and in what high esteem he held the office.

Indeed, the two men he revered most and whom he felt were most influential in his own life—A. J. Scott and F. D. Maurice—were both ministers, one a liberal charismatic Presbyterian, the other an Anglican.

If George MacDonald had merely pointed his finger accusatorially, without insight, without sensitivity, and without love for truth as his undergirding guide, then perhaps his words could be dismissed. But George MacDonald had a right to comment on the church, its function, and the state of those who lead it, because he spoke from within. He was no external finger-waving faultfinder, but a sore-hearted member of its ranks. He himself was a clergyman. He gave his life for the church, pastored in three or four locations, including temporary assignments, and preached throughout his life in hundreds of pulpits. He bore no grudges nor promoted any organizational agenda. He merely burned with the desire to see God's true church emerge glorious and triumphant.

No doubt MacDonald's heart-cry strikes such a deep root in my soul because of my own experience. Before I had ever heard of George MacDonald, before I had begun writing or editing or selling books, before my wife and I were married, the Lord gave us a burning vision of unity among God's people—a unity transcending denominational and doctrinal barriers. That vision has remained a focal point throughout the whole of our adult Christian lives and has never diminished.

At the time of its inception, we were actively involved in the life of our church and perceived that the fulfillment of that unity would occur in and through various churches and different denominational groups. Thus, as time went on, I gradually began to voice the deepening desire of my heart, that we as God's people were called to be one with our brothers and sisters in God, to the disregarding of doctrinal differences. I went so far even as to suggest that "the church" was not to be found in various buildings around town every Sunday morning, but that its true reality existed throughout the week as heart met heart.

Admittedly, I made blunders in my youthful attempt to communicate a message I felt God had shown me. But, I was yet unprepared for the strength with which those comfortable with existing church norms would resist the ideas I was attempting to communicate. I ultimately found myself cut off from the fellowship of many close spiritual friends, and spent several years floundering and alone, despondently reexamining many aspects of my faith.

Thank God, His sustaining hand comforted me, encouraged me, and gradually lifted me back to my feet, so that I could once again walk with confidence that He was indeed my Master. And He used George MacDonald in manifold ways during that critical period to rebuild my sorely bruised and wounded spiritual psyche.

Throughout all this, the vision of unity and of the church as a binding of hearts rather than a meeting in buildings never diminished. With more traditional doors closed, the Lord turned my attention in other directions as I sought a wider means to foster that unity among God's people. For twenty years that has been the founding priority of the ministry of our Christian bookstore, outweighing business and financial concerns. And now we find the fulfillment of that vision going forth through what we have undertaken with the works of George MacDonald, for wherever MacDonald's books go, they engender unity, and hearts are drawn together.

In George MacDonald we discovered one of like mind, a man who loved God's people as we did, one who desired something *more* for them. Thus, as over the years my wife and I found ourselves evaluating the whole concept of what *church* meant to us, we realized that George MacDonald was one of our closest and truest friends, a kindred spirit—in search of God's heart. So we read, we learned, we groped, we wept, and we prayed . . . and we grew with MacDonald toward a more expansive sense of God's design in our lives.

I have taken the liberty of this personal detour because over the years I have become aware that this search is a quest upon which many hungering hearts have embarked. Yet it is a path they must often walk alone, banished by misunderstanding and criticism of family and friends. It is my prayer, therefore, that MacDonald's words will be of encouragement and hope to such persons, as they have been to me.

It is out of this personal background that I came to *The Elect Lady* and discovered within its pages such a refreshingly simple yet courageously bold edict: "I don't believe that Jesus cares much for what is called the visible church. But he cares with his very Godhead for those that do as he tells them." I had followed MacDonald through many stories, and through the painful ups and downs of my own spiritual pilgrimage. Here, as he approached the end of his life, I found such a simple, unsophisticated tale in which he succinctly reveals his heart concerning unity and the church.

I find another feature of this new publication of *The Elect Lady* (retitled *The Landlady's Master* for the Bethany House series of reprinted MacDonald classics) personally significant. The original edition of this title is extremely rare and difficult to find. In sixteen years of searching for old MacDonald volumes, I had never so much as seen a single copy for sale through the rare book dealers with whom I had tracked the MacDonald *oeuvres*, and had resigned myself to never owning a copy. If I ever hoped to edit it for this series, I thought I would have to borrow a xeroxed reproduction from one of the MacDonald libraries.

As it happened, at a small gathering of MacDonald enthusiasts two years ago, some friends purchased a copy they had located through an antiquarian bookstore. It cost them, I think, something over $150, and I was speechless when they presented it as a gift to me. Who but a fellow bibliophile whose heart has been deeply touched by MacDonald could appreciate what I felt in that moment when my eyes fell on the hundred-year-old red cover inscribed *The Elect Lady*?

This little story, however, is bigger than a mere personal anecdote. In a deep and real sense, I think it typifies the very nature of how God is using George MacDonald in our own day—books being passed from hand to hand to hand, circulated and shared, friend to friend, father to son or daughter, child to parent, wife to husband, pastor to congregation . . . all over the world. It is impossible to predict the impact of any book that is loaned or given away. Truly the Lord multiplies many-hundredfold our feeble efforts on behalf of His kingdom. How beyond our imagining is His capacity to bring forth fruit from tiny beginnings.

It has been almost twenty years since a friend casually dropped in my hearing the name of an old Scottish author I'd never heard of. But as a result, over a million copies of George MacDonald books are back in print in five languages—and being circulated around the globe. A book you or I give away today could well prove the life-changing catalyst that starts tomorrow's man or woman of God on a path of growth and change which will result in untold millions experiencing a deeper walk with God.

So here I sit at this present moment with a single copy of *The Elect Lady* on the table in front of me—just *one* book, a rare title nearly impossible to find, its timeless truths locked away and inaccessible to large numbers of God's people. Yet out of this one book, a gift given to me by friends, will emerge this new edition; and by the time you are reading these words, ten, twenty, fifty, perhaps a hundred thousand copies will be in the hands of Christians the world over. That is the creative and multiplying power of God visibly at work! Truly, "unless a grain of wheat falls to the ground and dies, it remains only a single seed. But if it dies, it produces much fruit."

So thank you, my friends—you who are responsible for placing that copy of *The Elect Lady* in my hands two years ago so that it could now be shared with God's people. And thank you, Dave and Brenda Hiatt, for knowing my heart and for finding this book that so many will now be able to enjoy!

As a result of the publication of these editions of MacDonald's novels, a steady stream of inquiries has come my way from individuals wanting to obtain MacDonald's works in their original form. Unfortunately, I have had nothing encouraging to tell them, since the only means, until now, of locating the original full-length publications was through rare and antique book dealers, usually at prohibitive costs.

For years my goal has been to point a new generation of readers toward MacDonald—in any and *all* ways in which they can find his works. So I have bent my own efforts toward expanding the availability of MacDonald's books, not merely in one or two genres, but in all forms. I hope someday to see *all* his books available again in *both* edited and original form, as well as in easy-reading editions for young readers, and in various compilations and topical arrangements. I long to see a complete spectrum of MacDonald readily available for any reader, no matter what the age, the interest, or the reading level.

Toward that end, therefore, in addition to these edited editions from Bethany House, I have also been working on two other new groups of books. One, a series of essays and studies *about* MacDonald by various scholars who have studied his work. And, secondly, a new republication of MacDonald's books in their complete original format—not only the novels, but also his sermons, poems, essays, and stories. If you are interested either in reading about MacDonald or in tackling his books in their originals, please contact me for further information.

Michael Phillips
1707 E Street
Eureka, CA 95501

1 / Landlord's Daughter and Tenant's Son ____

The morning was of moderate warmth, not uncommon for that season, even so far north. Rising scents, mingling the fresh aromas of sun and rain and earth with grasses and grains and growing things, seemed suspended above the ground in an invisible cloud of olfactory pleasure. No breeze disturbed the fragrant vapor, nor carried it off, either toward the sea northward, or south to the mountains. Above the fields it hung, unheeded by those whose inner ears were asleep to the songs and stories the earth was telling, but giving inspiration and joy to the few poet-laborers of the region.

In truth, the latter did not comprise large numbers among the land's scant population. But what they lacked in force, such made up in imagination. As the Master said, the truths of the kingdom are hidden from the wise and revealed instead to children, for the last shall be first and the first last.

Indeed, the childlike are truly the inheritors of the earth. They who follow the Master of the race are, to those with eyes to see, exalted among men and women—though they dress in uncomely raiment, though their hands be soiled with the honest labor of the peasant, though their speech be quiet and unlearned, and though their appearance be the most humble.

In a kitchen of moderate size, flagged with slate, unassuming in its appointments, yet clearly looking more than a mere farmhouse, with the corner of a white pine table between them, sat two young people. They were evidently different in rank and were meeting upon a level other than friendship. It almost bore the appearance of a business meeting, though it was not business they were discussing. The one had in fact summoned the other that she might share several, as she thought, much-needed points out of the storehouse of her own wealth of knowledge, with one making his first, as she further thought, incomplete efforts toward self-expression. The young woman held in her hand a paper, which seemed the subject of their conversation.

She was about twenty-four or twenty-five, well grown and not ungraceful, with dark hair, dark hazel eyes, and rather large, handsome features, full of intelligence. It is true there was a slight look of hardness about her, almost regal—as such features must be, except after prolonged influence of a heart strong in self-subjugation. Her social expression mingled the gentle woman of education with the landlord's daughter, who was supreme over the household and its share in the labor of production. Attractive with the health of country life, there was nothing of the city's superficial refinement about her look or attire. Yet she clearly occupied a more dignified position in the social scale than he to whom she was speaking.

As to the young man, it would have required a deeper-seeing eye than falls to the lot of most observers not to take him for a weaker nature than the young woman. Indeed, the deference he showed her as the superior would have added to the difficulty of a true judgment. Appearance to the contrary notwithstanding, he was what could accurately be called a literary man. He had not been to college, but he had continued his studies to the extent his work made possible. He read widely, and he wrote better and better poetry—which he had done since childhood—with each passing year, even venturing now and then to send some of it to one or other of that northern region's newspapers or journals. He had not yet been published, nor had he made known his feeble attempts in that direction to the lady who was at this moment critically perusing his most recent effort. He was tall and thin, but plainly in fine health. He had a good forehead and clear green eyes, not too large or prominent, but full of light. His mouth was firm, and wore a curious smile in the midst of his sunburnt complexion. When perplexed he had a habit of pinching his upper lip between his finger and thumb, which at the present moment he was unconsciously indulging. He was the son of a small farmer—in what part of Scotland is of little consequence—and his companion for the moment was the daughter of the laird who owned the land he worked.

"I have read over the poem," said the young lady, "and it seems to me quite up to the average of what you see in print."

"I never suggested—indeed, never thought of trying to get it printed," replied the young man. "It is not the sort to attract an editor's attention."

"Of course. It was your mother who drew my attention to the verses."

"I must speak to my mother," responded the man in a meditative way.

"Surely you cannot object to someone seeing your work. She does not show it to everybody."

"This particular poem was never meant for any eyes but my own—except my brother's."

"What was the good of writing it if you didn't intend to show it to anyone?"

"The writing of it. But I wish it hadn't been *that* one my mother gave you to look at."

"Why?"

"It is not finished—as you will see when you read it more carefully. I have better ones, which someday perhaps an editor *will* look at with more—"

"I did see one line I thought hardly rhythmical," interrupted the lady."

"The lack of rhythm was intentional."

"That makes it even worse. Intention is the worst possible excuse for doing something wrong."

"I heartily agree. But in this case I would not grant that wrong has been done."

"The accent in a poem should always be made to fall in the right place."

"Then you face the danger of making the verse monotonous. Surely you know the difference between the letter of the law and the spirit of the law?"

"Of course. But religion has nothing to do with poetry, and the rule is strict."

"I have an idea that our great poets owe much of their music to the liberties they take with the rhythm. They treat the rule as its master, and break it when they see fit."

"You must be wrong there," interposed the laird's daughter. "And in any case, *you* cannot presume to take the liberties a great poet might take."

"It is a poor reward for being a great poet to be allowed to take liberties. There must be more to it than that."

Receiving no reply from the lady, the farmer's son continued.

"I should say that in doing their work to the best of their power, they were rewarded with the discovery of even higher laws of verse. Higher laws must always govern lower ones. The law of *meaning* is higher than the law of accents. Everyone must walk by the light given him. By the rules that others have laid down he may learn to walk; but once his heart is awake to truth, and his ear to measure, melody, and harmony, he must walk by the light and the music God gives him."

"That is dangerous doctrine, Andrew!" said the lady with a superior smile.

"Dangerous? Or merely a step or two out of the ordinary?"

"I won't debate the point. In any case, I will mark what faults I see in your poem and point them out to you."

"I am obliged to you," returned Andrew with his curious smile, hard to describe. It had in it a wonderful mixture of sweetness and humor, and a something that seemed to sit miles above his amusement. A heavenly smile it was, knowing too much to be angry. It had in it neither offense nor scorn. With respect to his poetry he was shy like a girl, but he showed no rejection of the patronage forced upon him by this lady.

He rose and stood a moment. "Well, Andrew, what is it?" she asked.

"When would you like me to call to pick up the verses?"

"In a week or so. By that time I shall have made up my mind what I think of them. If in doubt, I shall ask my father."

"I wouldn't like the laird to think I spend my time on poetry."

"You do write poetry, Andrew. A man should not do something he does not want to be known."

"That is true. I only feared an erroneous conclusion."

"My father knows you are a hard-working young man. There is not one of his farms in better order than yours. If it were otherwise, I should not be so interested in your poetry."

Andrew wished her less interested in it. To have his verses read was like having a finger poked in his eye. He had not known that his mother looked at the papers upon his desk, still less that she would have carried them to the daughter of the laird. But he showed little sign of his annoyance, bade the lady a pleasant morning, and left the kitchen.

Miss Fordyce followed him to the door and stood for a moment looking out. In front of her was a paved court, surrounded with low buildings, between two of which was visible, at the distance of a mile or so, a railway line where it approached a viaduct.

She heard the sound of an approaching train; and who, in a country place like that, where the rail line had only a few years before been laid down, could hear a train without looking up to see it go by?

2 / An Accident

While the two had been talking, a long train had been rattling through the dreary countryside.

For miles in any direction, nothing but hilly moorland was to be seen, a gathering of low hills, with now and then a higher one, broken by occasional torrents, in poor likeness of a mountain. No smoke proclaimed the presence of human dwelling. But there were spots between the hills where the hand of man had helped the birth of a feeble fertility. In front of the hills was a small but productive valley, on the edge of which stood the ancient house of Potlurg, with the heath behind it. Over a narrow branch of this valley spanned the viaduct, which the train was now approaching.

It was a slow train, with few passengers. Of these, a certain man was looking from his window with a vague, foolish sense of superiority, thinking what a forgotten and ugly country it seemed. He was a well-dressed, good-looking fellow, with keen but pale gray eyes, and a fine forehead, but a chin such as is held to indicate weakness. That should not be held against him in itself, however, for more than one of the strongest women I have known were defective in chin.

The young man was in the only first-class carriage of the nearly empty train, and was alone in it. Dressed in a gray suit, he was a little too particular in the smaller points of his attire, and lacked in consequence something of the look of a gentleman. Every now and then he would take off his hard round hat and pass a white left hand through his short-cut mousey hair, while his right caressed a far longer moustache in which he seemed inter-

ested. A certain indescribable heaviness and lack of light char-
acterized his pale face.

It was a lovely day in early June. The air had been rather cold
when the sun first made her appearance, but youth and health care
little about temperature on a holiday, with the sun shining, and
that sweetest sense—to such at least as are ordinarily bound by
routine—of having nothing to do. By now the countryside upon
which he looked out was warming with the advancing morning,
though he scarce paused to reflect upon the influences of nature
before his eyes, because he was of the leisure class. To many men
and women the greatest trouble is to choose, for self is the hardest
of masters to please; but as yet George Crawford had not been
troubled with much choosing.

Having left a crowded town behind, the loneliness he looked
upon was a pleasure to him, though he was incapable of seeing
the beauty in its lonely aspect. Compelled to spend time in it,
without the sense of only passing briefly through it, his own
company would soon have grown irksome to him. For however
much men may be interested in themselves, there are few indeed
who are interesting *to* themselves. Only those whose self is aware
of a higher presence can escape becoming disgusting bores to
themselves. That every man is endlessly greater than what he calls
himself must seem a paradox to the ignorant and dull, but a universe would be impossible without it. George had not arrived at
the discovery of this fact, and was yet for the present content with
both himself and his circumstances.

The heather was not in bloom, and the few flowers of the
heathy land made no show. Brown and darker brown predomi-
nated, with here and there a shadow of green. Weary of his outlook, George was settling back into his seat with his book when
suddenly there came a great crash and bang, followed by a tearing
sound.

He jumped up, but the same instant was thrown from his feet,
and all went black. For hours he knew no more.

Halfway through the train, one of the cars had jumped the

track, and the carriage in which George Crawford was riding had followed it. He had been thrown clear of the wreck as the carriage tumbled over, but one of his legs was broken.

"Papa! Papa! There has been an accident on the line!" cried Miss Fordyce, running into the laird's study, where he sat surrounded with books. "I saw it from the door!"

"Yes, I heard the crash. But hush," returned the old man, and listened. "I hear the train going on," he said after a moment.

"I am certain something terrible has happened," answered his daughter. "We must go and see if help is needed."

Before he had the chance to object, Alexa was out of the room, and in a moment more was running, in as straight a line as she could keep, across the heath to the low embankment. Andrew too had heard the crash as he walked home, and now caught sight of her running. He could not see the rail line, but convinced that something must be the matter, he turned and began running in the same direction.

For Alexa it was a hard and long run over the uneven ground. Troubled at the indifference she read on her father's face, she ran all the faster—too fast for thinking, but not too fast for the thoughts that came of themselves. What had become of her father? Since coming into the property, he had been growing less and less neighborly.

She had grabbed a bottle of brandy as she left the house, which impeded her running. Yet she made good speed, her dress gathered high in the other hand. Her long dark hair broken loose and flying in the wind, the assumed dignity she had displayed toward Andrew forgotten, and the only woman awake, she ran like a deer over the heather; and in little more than ten or twelve minutes, though it was a long moor-mile, she reached the embankment, flushed and panting.

Some of the carriages had rolled down, and the rails were a wreck. But the engine and half the train had been unharmed and had kept on; neither driver nor stoker was hurt, and they were hurrying to the nearby station to summon help. George Crawford lay at the foot of the bank insensible, with the guard of the train doing what he could to bring him back to consciousness. He was on his back, pale as death, making not the slightest motion, and scarce a sign of life about him.

Alexa tried to give him brandy, but she was so exhausted and her hand was shaking so from her run that she had to give the bottle to the guard. As healthy and strong as she was, she had to drag herself a little apart to sit down and catch her breath before she, too, fainted.

In the meantime, as the train approached the station, the driver, who belonged to the neighborhood, set his whistle shrieking wildly; and it was barely a matter of minutes before he had gotten word to the doctor, who set spurs to his horse and was galloping over the hills toward the scene. He first came upon Andrew trying to make Miss Fordyce swallow a little of the brandy to restore her dizzy head.

"There seems to be only one man hurt," the guard said to the doctor as he dismounted. "The young lady there ran so hard to come help that she dropped."

The doctor recognized Alexa and wondered what sort of reception her father would give the injured man. For he saw nowhere else but to Potlurg to take him. He turned toward the unconscious man and proceeded to do for him what he could without splints or bandages. Then, with the help of Andrew and the guard, and using pieces of the broken carriages, he constructed a sort of litter on which to carry him to the house.

"Is he dead?" asked Alexa from where she lay, coming back to herself.

"Not a bit of it," replied the doctor. "He's had a bad blow on the head, though, and his leg appears broken. We must get him somewhere as fast as we can."

"Do you know him?"

"No. But I don't know what else to do but take him to your house. It is closest by miles."

"Of course," said Alexa, standing again and approaching.

"You do not think it will bother the laird?"

"You scarcely know my father, Dr. Pratt."

"It would bother most people to have a wounded man quartered on them," returned the doctor. "It could be for weeks. Poor fellow! Not a bad looking chap either."

A fellow Scotsman who had been in the next carriage but had escaped almost unhurt now came up offering his service. Andrew and he took up the litter gently. They set out walking carefully, the doctor on one side, leading his horse, and Miss Fordyce on the other.

The strange procession took the whole of half an hour to reach their destination; and the house to which, after no small anxiety, they at last drew near was itself strange in its prospect. The features of the building itself were not so unusual had the gray stone structure been sitting in the middle of Aberdeen. But rising so suddenly out of the surrounding moorland of heather, broken only by a low stone wall and iron rail on one side that enclosed a grassy garden area with a hedge-lined walk and several trees, Potlurg was the most visible mark on the otherwise plain landscape for as far as the eye could see. From the elevated plot upon which the edifice stood, the ground sloped to the valley and was under careful cultivation. The entrance to the house was closed with a gate of wrought iron, of good workmanship, but so wasted with rust that it seemed on the point of vanishing. Here at one time had been the way into the house; but no door, and scarcely a window, was now to be seen on this side of the building. It was very old and consisted of three levels, out from the top of which projected three gables. A second building, a later addition, sat behind the main house, both of which were made entirely of the quarried granite so plentiful to the region, and roofed in black slate.

Crawford had begun to recover consciousness, but when he came to himself, he was received by acute pain. The least attempt to move was torture, and again he fainted.

3 / The Laird

Conducted by the lady, they passed round the front to the side of the house fronting the garden, and across the court to a door in the very middle below the center gable. It was not a huge door but large enough for the man that stood there—a little man, with colorless face and a quiet, abstracted look. His eyes were cold and keen, his features small, delicate, and regular. He had an erect little back and was dressed in a long-tailed coat, looking not much like a laird as he stood framed in the gray stone wall, in which windows here and there at varying heights and distances revealed a wonderful arrangement of floors and rooms inside.

"Good morning, Mr. Fordyce!" said the doctor. "A bad accident, I suppose you have heard, but it might have been worse. Only this one man was injured."

The laird spoke no word of objection or welcome. They carried the unconscious fellow into the house, following its mistress to a room, where, with the help of her one domestic, and instructed by the doctor, she soon had a bed prepared for him. Then the doctor left them and rode away at full speed to fetch the appliances necessary, leaving the laird standing by the bed with a look of mild dissatisfaction but not a whisper of opposition to the proceedings.

They had carried George Crawford to the guest chamber, a room far more comfortable than a stranger might have believed possible from the austere look of the house. Everything in it was old-fashioned and not exactly in apple pie order. But it was rapidly and silently restored to its humble ideal, and when the doctor returned with his assistant after an incredibly brief absence, he seemed both surprised and pleased at the change.

"He must have someone to sit with him, Miss Fordyce," he instructed after they had completed setting and splinting the leg.

"I will myself," she answered. "But you must give me exact directions, for I have done no nursing."

"If you will come outside and walk with me for a moment," said the doctor, "I will tell you all you need to know."

They left the room and went outside. "I think he will sleep now," Dr. Pratt resumed, "at least for part of the afternoon. It is not a very awkward fracture," he went on. "It might have been much worse. We shall have him about in a few weeks. But while the bones are uniting, he will need the greatest care, and he must not move about under any circumstances."

While they were walking and talking outside, the laird turned away from the sick-chamber and returned to his study. There he walked up and down, lost and old and pale, looking the very incarnation of the room with its ancient volumes all around. Whatever his eyes fell upon he turned from as if he no longer had any pleasure in it. Presently he stole back to the room where the sufferer lay, still asleep. His daughter and the doctor had not returned yet.

On tiptoe, with a caution suggestive of approaching a wild beast asleep, the laird crept to the bed, looked down on his unwelcome guest with an expression of sympathy crossed with dislike, and shook his head slowly and solemnly, like one injured but forgiving.

His eye fell on the young man's pocketbook. It had fallen from his coat as they undressed him, and now lay on a table by the bedside. He picked it up just before Alexa reentered.

"How is he, Father?" she asked.

"He is fast asleep," answered the laird. "How long does the doctor think he will have to be here?"

"I did not ask him," she replied.

"That was an oversight, my child," he returned. "It is important we should know the moment he can be removed."

"We shall know it in good time. The doctor called it an affair of weeks—or months—I forget. But you shall not be troubled, Father. I will attend to him."

"But I *am* troubled, Alexa! You do not know how little money I have!" Again he left, went to his study, shut the door, locked it, and began to search the pocketbook. He found certain banknotes and made a discovery as well concerning its owner.

With the help of Meg, her old servant, Alexa noiselessly continued to make the chamber more comfortable, while Crawford lay in a half slumber. Chintz curtains veiled the windows, which, in spite of being rather narrow, had admitted too much light. An old carpet deadened the sound of footsteps on the creaking floorboards—for the bones of a house do not grow silent with age. A fire burned in the antique grate, and was a soul to the chamber which was chilly, looking to the north, with walls so thick that it took half the summer to warm them through.

Old Meg, moving to and fro, kept shaking her head like her master as if she also were in the secret of some house misery. But she was only indulging the funereal temperament of an ancient woman.

As Alexa ran through the heather that morning, she looked not altogether unlike a peasant; her shoes were strong, her dress was short. But now she came and went in a soft-colored gown, neither ill-made nor unbecoming, and her bearing was much different. She did not seem to belong to what is commonly called society, but she looked dignified at times, at times almost stately, with an expression of superiority, not strong enough to make her handsome face unpleasing. It resembled her father's, but, for a woman's, was cast in a larger mold.

The day crept on.

The invalid was feverish. His nurse obeyed the doctor minutely. She had her tea brought to her, but when the supper hour arrived, she went to join her father.

They always ate in the kitchen. Strange to say, in one so old and so large, there was no dining room in the house. At least none to which that purpose seemed intended, though there was a sweet old-fashioned drawing room. The servant remained with the sufferer, eating her porridge and milk. The laird partook but sparingly, on the ground that the fare tended toward fatness, which affliction of age he congratulated himself on having hitherto escaped.

They ate in silence, but not a glance of her father that might indicate a want escaped the daughter. When the meal was ended and the old man had given thanks, Alexa put on the table a big black Bible, which her father took with solemn face and reverent gesture. It was their custom to read aloud from it every night; and in the course of his reading of the New Testament, he had come to the twelfth chapter of St. Luke, with the Lord's parable of the rich man whose soul was required of him. He read it beautifully, with an expression that seemed to indicate a sense of the Lord's meaning what he said.

"We will omit the psalm this evening—for the sake of the sufferer," he said, having ended the chapter. "The Lord will have mercy and not sacrifice."

They rose from their chairs and knelt on the stone floor. The old man prayed with much tone and expression, and I think meant all he said, though none of it seemed to spring from fresh need or new thankfulness, for he used only the old stock phrases, which flowed freely from his lips. He dwelt much on the merits of the Savior; he humbled himself as the chief of sinners, whom it must be a satisfaction to God to cut off, but a greater satisfaction to spare for the sake of one whom the Lord loved. Plainly the laird counted it a most important thing to stand well with him who had created man.

When they rose Alexa looked formally solemn, but the wan face of her father looked better than before: the psyche of his being, if not the ego, had prayed—and felt comfortable. He sat down and looked fixedly as if into eternity, but perhaps it was into vacancy; they are much the same to most people.

At length he rose and said, "Come into the study for a moment, Lexy, if you please." His politeness to his daughter, and indeed to all that came near him, was one of the most notable points in his behavior.

Alexa followed the black, slender, erect little figure up the staircase, which consisted of about a dozen steps, filling the entrance from wall to wall, a width of about twelve feet. Between it and the outer door there was but room for the door of the kitchen on the one hand and that of a small closet on the other. At the top was a wide space, a sort of irregular hall, more like an out-of-door court, paved with large flat stones into which projected the other side of the rounded mass, bordered by the grassy enclosure.

The laird turned to the right, and through a door into a room that had but one small window hidden by bookcases. It smelled musty, of old books and decayed bindings, an odor not unpleasant to some nostrils. He closed the door behind him, placed a chair for his daughter, and set himself in another beside a table, upon which were stacked books and papers.

"This is a sore trial, Alexa," he said with a sigh.

"It is indeed, Father—for the poor young man!" she returned.

"True. But it is a more serious matter to us than you seem to think. It will cost much more to keep the fellow here than, in the present state of my finances, I can afford to bear."

"But, Father," said Alexa, "we could not help what happened. We must take the luck as it comes."

"Alexa," rejoined the laird with solemnity, "there is no such thing as luck. It was either for the young man's sins, or to prevent worse, or for necessary discipline that the train was overturned. The cause is known to *Him*. Everything is in his hands."

"Then if what you say is true, Father, our part in the incident was ordered too. So we must receive our share of the trouble as from the hand of the Lord."

"Certainly, my dear. It was the expense I was thinking of. I was only lamenting—I was not opposing—the will of the Lord. A man's natural feelings remain."

"If the thing is not to be helped, let us think no more about it."

"It is the expense, my dear! I am doing my utmost to impress the seriousness of the situation upon you. Next to the grace of God, money is the thing hardest to get and hardest to keep. If we are not wise with it, the grace—I mean money—will not go far."

"Not so far as the next world anyhow," said Alexa as if to herself.

"Please, child! The Redeemer tells us to make friends of the mammon of unrighteousness, that when we die it may receive us into everlasting habitations."

"I read the passage recently, Father, and I have heard that it ought to be translated 'make friends *by means of* the mammon of unrighteousness,' so that *they* not *it* will receive you. It is the friendships with people that last, Father, certainly not friendship with mammon."

Alexa had reason to fear that her father had made a friend of, and never a friend *with*, the use *of* his money. At the same time, the halfpenny he put in the plate every Sunday must go a long way if it was not estimated, like that of the poor widow, according to the amount he possessed, but according to the difficulty he found in parting with it.

"You know we must not lightly change even the translated word. But in any case," resumed the laird, "after weeks, perhaps months of nursing and food and medical supplies, he will walk away and we shall not see so much as a pound of the money he has with him. Our money will have vanished, I tell you, as a tale that is told."

"The little it will cost you, Father—"

"The little! Hold there, my child! It will cost—that is enough! You cannot know how much it will cost me, for you do not know what money stands for in my eyes."

"I have a little money of my own," Alexa returned. "I will pay the expenses and it shall cost you nothing. What would you do, tell him his friends must pay his board or else come to take him away? A nice anecdote that would be in the annals of the Fordyces of Potlurg!"

"His friends must in any case be notified," rejoined her father. "I learned from his pocketbook—"

"Father!"

"I have a right to know whom I receive under my roof, Alexa. Besides, I have learned thereby that the youth has a sort of connection with us."

"You don't mean it!"

"I do mean it. His mother and yours were first cousins."

"That is hardly a casual connection. It is a close kinship. All the more we owe it to keep him here. But I give you my word, you shall have nothing more to worry about concerning the expenses."

She bade her father good night, then returned to the bedside of the patient and released Meg.

4 / The Laird and the Cousins

Thomas Fordyce was a sucker from the root of a very old family tree. Born in poverty, with great pinching on the parts of father and mother, brothers and sisters, he had been educated for the church. But from pleasure in scholarship, from archaeological tastes, a passion for the arcane of history, and a love of literature, strong although not of the highest kind, he had settled down as a schoolmaster, and in his calling had reasonably excelled. By all who knew him he was regarded as an accomplished, amiable, and worthy man.

When his years were verging on the undefined close of middle age, he saw the lives between him and the family property, one by one, wither at the touch of death until at last there was no one but him and his daughter to succeed. At that time he was the head of a flourishing school in a large manufacturing town, and it was not without some regret, though with more pleasure, that he yielded his profession and retired to the family estate of Potlurg, which was now his.

Greatly dwindled as he found the property, and much and long as it had been mismanaged, it was yet of considerable value and worth a wise care. The result of the labor he spent upon it was such that it had now for years yielded him, if not a large rental income, one far larger at least than his daughter imagined. But the sinking of the schoolmaster in the laird seemed to work ill for the man and good only for the land.

I say *seemed* because what we call degeneracy is often but the unveiling of what was there all the time, and the evil we could

34

become, we are. If I have in me the tyrant or the miser, there he is, and such am I—as surely as if the tyrant or the miser were even now visible to the wondering dislike of my neighbors. I do not say the characteristic is so strong, or would be so hard to change as what its revealing development shows it must become. But it is there, alive, as an egg is alive, and by no means inoperative like a mere germ, but exercising real, though occultic, influence on the rest of my character. Therefore, except the growing vitality be in the process of killing these ova of death, it is for the good of the man that they should be so far developed as to show their existence. If the man does not then starve and slay them, they will drag him to the judgment seat of a fiery indignation.

For the laird, nature could ill replace the human influences that had surrounded the schoolmaster; while enlargement both of means and leisure enabled him to develop by indulgence a passion for a peculiar kind of possession, which, however refined in its objects, was yet but a branch of the worship of Mammon. It suits the enemy just as well, I presume, that a man should give his soul for coins or books or jewelry or golden objects or any other such things as for money in a bank account.

In consequence, Mr. Fordyce was growing more and more withdrawn, ever filling less the part of a man—which was intended to be a hiding place from the wind, a covert from the tempest. He was more and more for himself, and thereby losing his life. Dearly as he loved his daughter, he was, by slow fallings away, growing ever less of a companion, less of a comfort, less of a necessity to her, and requiring less and less of her for the good or ease of his existence.

We wrong those near us in being independent of them. God himself would not be happy without his Son. We ought to lean on each other, giving and receiving—not as weaklings, but as lovers. Love is strength as well as need.

On Alexa's part, she was more able to live alone than most women. Therefore this downward progression of her father was the worse for her. Too satisfied with herself, too little uneasy when alone, she did not know that by herself she was not in good enough company. She was what most would call a strong nature, and had not an inkling that weaknesses belong to and grow out of such a strength as hers.

The distant scions of a family tree are often those who make the most of it. The schoolmaster's daughter knew more about the Fordyces of Potlurg and cared more for their traditions than any who of past years had reaped its advantages or shared its honors. Interest in the channel down which one has slid into the world is reasonable, and may even be elevating. But with Alexa it passed beyond good and worked against the development of her character. Proud of a family with a history, and one occasionally noted in the annals of the country, she regarded herself as the superior of all with whom she had hitherto come into contact. To the poor, to whom she was invariably kind, she was less condescending than to such as came nearer her own imagined standing. With both, however, she was constantly aware that she belonged to the elect of the land.

But society took its revenge—the rich tradespeople looked down upon her as only a schoolmaster's daughter. Against their arrogance her indignation buttressed her lineal with her mental superiority. In the final accounting, the pride of family is little more than a personal arrogance. And now at length she was in her natural position as heiress of Potlurg!

She was what many persons consider "religious"—if one may be called religious who felt no immediate relation to the source of her being. She felt bound to defend, so far as she honestly could, the doctrines concerning God and his ways transmitted by the elders of her people. But this, and little more, was all her religion toward God amounted to. Yet at the same time she had a strong sense of obligation to do what was right.

Her father gave her so little money to spend on managing the household that she had to be very careful with her housekeeping, and they lived in the humblest way. She troubled him as little as she could, believing him from the half statements and hints he gave, and his general carriage toward life, that he was indeed oppressed by lack of money. She little suspected his true state, nor the difficulties he induced by himself. Over the years it had come to be understood between them that the income of the poultry yard was Alexa's own. She watched over it carefully, increased her quantity of fowl, sold their eggs, and gradually managed to gather for herself some little store against the future. It was to this she now mainly trusted for the requirements of her invalid. Her father could hardly object to the proceeding, though he did not like her having even so modest an independent means; he felt what was hers ought to be his far more than he felt what was his was also hers.

Alexa had not learned to place value on money beyond its use, but she was not therefore free from the service of Mammon. She looked to it as a power essential, not derived. She did not see it as God's creation but merely as an existence, thus making of a creature of God's design the Mammon of unrighteousness. She did not, however, cling to it, but was ready to spend it if the occasion presented itself. At the same time, had George Crawford looked less handsome or less of a gentleman, she would not have been quite so ready to devote the contents of her little secret drawer to his recovery.

The discovery of her relationship to the young man waked a new feeling. She had never had a brother, never known a cousin, and had avoided the approach of such young men who, of inferior position in her eyes, had sought to be friendly with her. Now here was one thrown helpless on her care, with necessities enough to fill the gap between his real relation to her and that of the brother after whom she had sighed in vain. It was a new and delightful sensation to have a family claim on a young man—a claim, the material advantage of which was all on his side, the devotion all on hers. She found herself invaded by a flood of tenderness toward the man. Was he not her cousin, a gentleman, and helpless as any newborn child? Nothing should be wanting that a strong woman could do for a powerless man!

George Crawford was in excellent health when the accident occurred, and so when he began to recover, his restoration was rapid. The process, however, still took long enough so that the cousins discovered more of each other than twelve months of ordinary circumstances would have made possible.

George felt neither the need nor the joy of the new relationship so much as Alexa, and disappointed her by the coolness of his response to her revelation of their kinship. As they were both formal—that is, less careful as to the reasonable than the conventional—they were not very ready to fall in love. Such people may learn all about each other and not come near enough for love to be possible. Some people approximate at once, and at once decline to love, remaining friends the rest of their lives. Others love instantly. Still others take a whole married life to come near enough—and at last love. But the reactions of need and ministration can hardly fail to breed tenderness and disclose the best points of character.

The cousins were both handsome, and—which was of more consequence—each thought the other handsome. They found their religious opinions very similar—which was little wonder, for they had gone for years to the same church every Sunday, had been regularly pumped upon from the same reservoir, and had drunk the same arguments concerning things true and untrue.

George found that Alexa had plenty of brains, a cultivated judgment, and some knowledge of literature. There was in fact no branch of science with which she did not have some acquaintance, and in which she did not take some interest. Her father's teaching was beyond any he could have procured for her, and what he taught she had learned, for she had a love of knowing, a tendency to growth, a capacity for seizing real points, though as yet perceiving next to nothing of their relation to human life and hope. She believed herself a good judge of poetic verse, but in truth her knowledge of poetry was limited to its outer forms, of which she had made good studies with her father. She had learned the *how* before the *what,* knew the body before the soul—could tell good binding but not bad leather—in a word, knew verse but not poetry.

She understood nothing of music, but George did not miss that. He was more sorry she did not know French—not for the sake of reading its literature, but because of showing herself an educated woman.

Diligent in business, not fervent in spirit, she was never idle. But there are other ways than idleness of wasting time. Alexa was continually striving toward what is called "improving herself," but it was a big phrase for a small matter. She had not learned that to do the will of God is the way to improve oneself. She would have scorned the narrowness of any who told her so, not understanding what the will of God means.

She found that her guest and cousin was a man of some position, and wondered why her father had never mentioned the relationship previously. The fact was that, in a time of poverty, the schoolmaster had requested from George's father a small loan without security, and the banker had behaved as a rich banker to a poor relation.

George occupied a place of trust in his father's bank, and, though not yet admitted to a full knowledge of its more important transactions, hoped soon to be made a partner.

When George's father came to Potlurg to see his son, the laird declined to appear, and the banker contented himself thereafter with Alexa's letters concerning his son's condition.

Weeks went by, then a month. George's recovery was steady but slow; only time could repair the broken bone. After six weeks he began to hobble feebly about once or twice a day with the help of a cane. Alexa's money was nearly exhausted, and most of her chickens had been devoured by the flourishing convalescent. But not yet would the doctor allow him to return to business.

One night the electric condition of the atmosphere made it heavy and sultry, and George could not sleep. The evening was well advanced into night when suddenly a bannered spear of vividest lightning seemed to lap the house in its flashing folds, and a simultaneous terrible burst of thunder was mingled, as it seemed, with the fall of some part of the building.

George sat up in bed and listened.

All was still. He thought to himself that he should rise and see what had happened and whether anyone was hurt. He might meet Alexa, and a talk with her would be a pleasant episode in his sleepless night. He rose slowly out of the bed, got into his dressing gown and, taking his stick, walked softly from the room.

His door opened immediately on the top of the stair. He stood and listened, but was aware of no sequel to the noise. Another flash came and lighted up the space around him, with its walls of many angles. When the darkness returned, but while the thunder yet bellowed, he caught the glimmer of a light under the door of the study and made his way toward it over the worn slabs of floorboard.

He knocked, but there was no answer.

He pushed the door and saw that the light came from behind a projecting bookcase. He hesitated a moment and glanced about him.

A little clinking sound came from somewhere.

He stole nearer the source of the light. What if a thief was in the house! He peeped round the end of the bookcase. With his back to him, the laird was kneeling before an open chest. He had just counted a few pieces of gold and was putting them away. Hearing the soft footstep, he looked over his shoulder, his face deathly pale, his eyes for a moment blank. Then with a shivering smile he rose. He had a thin, worn dressing gown over his night-shirt, and looked but the thread of a man.

"You take me for a miser?" he said, trembling, and stood expecting an answer.

Crawford was bewildered. What business could the laird be about at such a time of night?

"I am *not* a miser!" resumed the laird. "A man may count his money without being a miser!"

He stood and stared, still trembling, at his guest, either too much startled or too gentle to find fault with his intrusion. George did not know what to think.

"I beg your pardon, laird," said George at last. "I knocked, but receiving no answer, I feared something was wrong."

"But why are you out of bed—and you an invalid?" returned Mr. Fordyce.

"I heard a heavy fall and feared the lightning had done some damage."

"We shall see about that in the morning. In the meantime, we had better go to bed," said the laird.

They turned together toward the door.

"What a multitude of books you have, Mr. Fordyce!" remarked George. "I had not a notion of such a library in the county."

"I have been a lover of books all my life," returned the laird. "And they continue to gather as the years pass."

"It must be your love that draws them," replied George.

"I think the storm is over," remarked the laird.

He did not tell his guest that there was scarcely a book on those shelves that was not considered rare and not sought after by book buyers—not a single title that was not worth money in the book market. Here and there the dulled gold of a fine antique binding returned the gleam of the candle, but any gathering of old law or worthless divinity volumes would have looked much the same.

"I should like to glance over them sometime," said George. "There must be some valuable volumes among so many."

"Rubbish! Merely rubbish!" rejoined the old man testily, almost hustling the guest from the room. "I am ashamed to hear it called a library."

Later, as he again lay awake in his bed, it seemed to Crawford an altogether strange incident. Certainly a man may count his money when he pleases, he thought, but not the less must it seem odd that he should do so in the middle of the night, and with such a storm flashing and roaring around him, apparently unheeded.

The next morning he got his cousin to talk about her father, but drew from her nothing to cast light on what he had seen.

5 / In the Garden

Of the garden that had been the pride of many owners of the place, only a small portion remained. It was strangely antique, haunted with a beauty both old and wild, the sort of garden for the children of heaven to play in when men sleep.

In a little arbor constructed by an old man who had seen the garden grow less and less through successive generations, under a tent of honeysuckle in a cloak of fragrant and many-colored sweet peas, sat George and Alexa, two highly respectable young people, Scots of Scotland, like Jews of Judea, well satisfied of their own worthiness. How they found their talk interesting, I can scarcely think. I should have expected them to be driven by very dullness to thoughts and talk of love. But the one was too prudent to initiate it, the other too staid to entice it. Yet, as people on the borders of love are on the borders of poetry, they had begun talking about a certain new poem, concerning which, having read several reviews of it, George had an opinion.

"You should tell my father your thoughts, George," suggested Alexa; "he is the best judge I know."

She did not understand that it was little more than the grammar of poetry the schoolmaster had ever given himself to understand. His best criticism was to show phrase calling to phrase across gulfs of speech.

The little iron gate, whose hinges were almost gone with rust, creaked and gnarred as it slowly opened to admit the approach of a young countryman. He advanced with the long, slow, heavy step suggestive of nailed shoes, but his green eyes had an outlook like that of an eagle from its aerie, and seemed to dominate his being, originating rather than directing his motions. He had a russet-colored face, much freckled, hair so dark red as to be almost brown, a large, well-shaped nose, a strong chin, and a mouth of sweetness whose smile was peculiarly its own, having in it at once the mystery and revelation of the young man known as Andrew Ingram. As he drew near, he took off his cap and held it as low as his knee, then stood waiting with something of the air of an old-fashioned courtier. His clothes, all but his coat, which was of some blue stuff, and his Sunday one, were of a large-ribbed corduroy. For a moment no one spoke. His cheeks colored a little, but he kept silent, his eyes on the lady.

"Good morning, Andrew," she said at length. "There was something you were going to call about, I forget what. Remind me—will you?"

"I did not come before, ma'am, because I knew you were occupied. And even now it does not greatly matter."

"Oh, I remember!—the poem! I am very sorry, but I had so much to think about that it entirely slipped my mind."

For an instant, an expression half-amused, half-shy, without a trace of embarrassment, shadowed the young man's face.

"I wish you would let me have the verses back, ma'am. I should be very obliged to you," he said.

"Well, I admit they might first be improved before I go any further with them. I read them one evening to my father, and he agreed with me that two or three of the lines were not quite rhythmical. But he said it was a fair attempt, and for a working man very creditable."

What Andrew was thinking, it would have been hard to gather from his smile; but I believe it was that if he himself had read the verses aloud, the laird would have found no fault with their rhythm. His carriage seemed more that of a patient, respectful amusement than anything else.

Alexa rose, but then resumed her seat.

"As the poem is a religious one, there can be no harm in

handing it to you Sunday after church," she remarked; "—that is," she added meaningfully, "if you will be there."

"Give it to Dawtie, if you please, Miss Fordyce," replied Andrew.

"Ah," returned Alexa, in a tone almost of rebuke.

"I seldom go to church," said Andrew, reddening a little, but losing no sweetness from his smile.

"I have heard that. It is wrong of you not to be regular. Why don't you go to church?"

Andrew was silent.

"I want you to tell me," persisted Alexa, with a peremptoriness she had inherited from the schoolmaster. She had known Andrew too as a pupil of her father's.

"If you insist, ma'am," replied Andrew. "I not only learn nothing from Mr. Smith, but I think that much of what he says is not true."

"Still you ought to go for the sake of example."

"Do wrong to make other people follow my example! How could that be right?"

"Wrong to go to church! What *do* you mean? Wrong to pray with your fellow Christians?"

"Perhaps the time may come when I shall be able to pray with them, even though the words they use seem addressed to a tyrant, not to the Father of Jesus Christ. But at present I cannot. I might endure to hear Mr. Smith say evil things concerning God, but the evil things he says to God make me quite unable to pray, and I would feel like a hypocrite to attempt it in such a setting."

"Whatever you may think of Mr. Smith's doctrines, it is presumptuous to set yourself up as too good to go to church."

"My difficulties with the church have nothing to do with thinking myself good, ma'am, which I do not. But I must bear the reproach. I cannot consent to be a hypocrite in order to avoid being called one."

Either Miss Fordyce had no answer to this, or did not choose to give any. She was not so much troubled that Andrew would not go to church. Like many who feel compelled to debate on matters religious, she was arguing on behalf of the traditions of men rather than from the depth of her own personal religious convictions. In truth, what offended her most was the unhesitating decision with which the unlearned young man set her counsel aside. Andrew made her a respectful bow, turned away, put on his cap, which he had held in his hand all the time, and passed through the garden gate.

"Who is the fellow?" asked George, partaking sympathetically of his companion's annoyance.

"He is Andrew Ingram, the son of a small farmer, one of my father's tenants. He and his brother work with their father on the farm. They are quite respectable people."

"He a tenant and you his mistress, yet he talks to you so!"

"Andrew is conceited, but he has his good points. He imagines himself a poet, and indeed his work has merit. The worst of him is that he sets himself up as better than other people."

"A common fault with the self-educated."

"He does go on educating himself, I believe, but he had a good start to begin with. My father took great pains with him at school. He helped to carry you here after the accident—and would have taken you to his father's place if I would have let him."

George cast on her a look of gratitude.

"Thank you for keeping me," he said. "But still, I should have taken some notice of his kindness."

6 / Andrew and Sandy Ingram_____

Of the persons in my narrative, Andrew Ingram is the simplest, therefore the hardest, to be understood by an ordinary reader. In order to get at the foundation of his character, I must take up his history from a certain point in his childhood many years before these present events.

One summer evening, he and his brother Sandy were playing together on a knoll in one of their father's fields. Andrew was ten years old and Sandy a year younger. The two quarreled, the spirit of ancestral borderers woke in them, and they fell to blows.

The younger was the stronger for his years, and they punched each other with relentless vigor, when suddenly they heard a voice. They stopped their fight, and saw before them a humble-looking man with a pack on his back. He was a peddler, known and noted for his honesty and his silence, but the boys had never laid eyes upon him; to them he was a stranger.

They stood abashed before him, dazed with the blows they had received, and ashamed of themselves; for they had been well brought up, their mother being an honest disciplinarian and their father never interfering with what she judged right. It was not their custom to argue and fight, and somehow the sight of the old man brought them to their senses.

The sun was setting near the horizon, and shone with level rays full on the peddler, but when the boys thought of him afterward, they seemed to remember more light in his face than that of the sun. Their conscience bore him witness and his look awed them. Involuntarily they turned from him, seeking refuge with each other: his eyes shone so, they said. But then immediately they turned back to look at him again.

Sandy knew the pictures in *Pilgrim's Progress,* and Andrew had read it through more than once. Therefore, when they saw the man had an open book in his hand, and heard him, standing there in the sun, begin to read from it, the first thing to come to their minds was that it must be Christian, waiting for the Evangelist to come.

It is impossible to say how much is fact and how much imagination in what children recollect. The one must almost always supplement the other. But the boys were quite sure that the words he read were: "And lo, I am with you always, even to the end of the world!" The next thing they remembered was their walking slowly down the hill in the red light of the setting sun, and all at once waking up to the fact that the man was gone, they did not know when or where. But their arms were round one another and they were full of a strange awe. Then Andrew saw something red on Sandy's face.

"Eh, Sandy!" he cried, "it's blood!" and he burst into tears.

It was, in fact, his own blood, not Sandy's—the discovery of which fact relieved Andrew, and did not so greatly discompose Sandy, who was less sensitive. But the sight of the blood woke still deeper feelings of conscience within them.

They began at length to speculate on what had happened. One thing was clear—it was because they were fighting that the man had come. But it was not so clear who the man was. He could not be Christian, because Christian went over the river. Andrew suggested it might have been Evangelist, for he seemed to be always about. Sandy added as his contribution to the idea that he might have picked up Christian's bundle and been carrying it home to his wife. They came to the conclusion in the end, however, by no process of logical reasoning, I think, but by a conviction, which the idea itself brought with it, that the stranger was the Lord himself, and that the pack on his back was their sins, which he was carrying away to throw out of the world.

"Eh, wasn't it fearful he should come by just when we was fighting!" said Sandy.

"Eh, but it's good he did! We might have been at it yet. But we won't now—will we ever again, Sandy?"

"No, that we won't."

"He said, 'Lo, I am with you always!' " continued Andrew. "And even suppose he weren't, we wouldn't dare do behind his back what we wouldn't do before his face."

"Do you really think it *was* him, Andrew?"

"Well," replied Andrew, "if the devil goes about like a roaring lion seeking who he can devour, as Father says, it's not likely *He* wouldn't be going about as well, seeking to hold him off us."

"Ay," said Sandy.

They were silent a minute. Then at last the elder spoke again. "And so now," he proposed, "what do you suppose we are to do?"

For Andrew, whom both father and mother judged the dreamiest of mortals, was in reality one of the most practical beings in the whole parish. To him, every truth must be accompanied by some corresponding act. If any of my readers say he was too young to take spiritual things so seriously, I reply by asking if the fact that so few children do take the Lord's words to heart be justification for discounting what he himself prayed when he said, "I thank thee, O Father, because thou hast hid these things from the wise and learned, and revealed them to little children." Truly Andrew and Sandy were unusual children in what followed, but unusual because they were *more* what children were intended to be, not *less*; more childlike, therefore nearer the heart of God. As Andrew grew through the years, by and by people began to mock him, calling him nothing but a poet and a heretic, because he constantly sought to *do* the things that they said they believed. Most unpractical must every man appear who genuinely believes in the things that are unseen. The man called practical by the men of this world is he who busies himself building his house on the sand, while he does not even acknowledge a lodging in the inevitable beyond for which he needs to prepare.

"What are we going to do?" repeated Andrew. "If the Lord is going about like that, looking after us, we've surely got something to do looking after him!"

Sandy did not have a ready answer. And it was a good thing, with the reticence of children, that neither thought of bringing up the affair and laying the case of the question before their parents; the traditions of the elders would have ill agreed with the doctrine of obedience the sons were now under.

Suddenly one day it came into Andrew's mind that the Bible they read at church, to which he had never paid much attention, told all about Jesus. *There* must be the answer to his question!

He began at the beginning and grew so interested in the stories that he forgot why he had begun to read them. But at length it dawned on him that nothing he had read told anything about the man who was going up and down the world, gathering up their sins and carrying them away in his pack. He turned to the New Testament to see if there might be something in that book about Jesus Christ. Here also it was well they asked no advice, for they would probably have been directed to the Epistle to the Romans, with explanations yet more foreign to the heart of Paul than false to his Greek. They began to read the story of Jesus as told by his friend Matthew, and when they had ended it, went on to the gospel according to Mark. But they had not read far when Sandy cried out, "Eh, Andrew, it's all just the same thing over again!"

"Not altogether," answered Andrew. "Let's go on and see."

Finally Andrew came to the conclusion that it was close enough to the same thing that he would rather go back and read the other again, for the sake of some particular things he remembered he wanted to make sure about. So they went back and read St. Matthew a second time, and came eventually to these words:

If two of you shall agree on earth as touching anything that they shall ask, it shall be done for them of my Father which is in heaven.

"There's two of us here!" cried Andrew, laying down the book. "Let's try it!"

"Try what?" asked Sandy. His brother read the passage again.

"Let the two of us ask him for something!" concluded Andrew. "What will it be?"

"I wonder if it means only once, or maybe three times, like the three wishes," suggested Sandy, who, like most Christians, would rather have a talk about it than do what he was told.

"We might ask for what would not be good for us," returned Andrew.

"And make fools of ourselves," assented Sandy, with the story of *The Three Wishes* in his mind.

"Do you think he would give it us, then?"

"I don't know."

"But," pursued Andrew, "if we were so foolish as that old man and woman, it would be better to find out, and begin to grow wise. I'll tell you what we'll do, we'll make it our first wish to know what's best to ask for, and then we can go on asking!"

"Yes, that's it."

"I fancy we'll have as many wishes as we like! Down on your knees, Sandy."

They kneeled together.

I fear there will be many who say, "How ill-instructed the poor children were—actually mingling the gospel and fairy tales!"

"Happy children," I say, "who could blunder into the very heart of the will of God concerning them, and *do* the thing immediately that the Lord taught them, using the common sense which God had given and the fairy tale had nourished!" The Lord of the promise is the Lord of all true parables and all good fairy tales.

Andrew prayed:

"Oh, Lord, tell Sandy and me what to ask for. We're unanimous."

They got up from their knees. They had said what they had to say, why say more?

They felt rather dull. Nothing came to them. The prayer was

prayed, and they could make out no answer. They put the Bible away in a rough box where they kept it among rose-leaves— ignorant priests of the lovely mystery of him who was with them always—and without a word went each his own way. Andrew was disconsolate the rest of the day. They had prayed and nothing had come of it, and he did not know what to do.

In the evening, while it was yet light, Andrew went alone to the elder tree, where it was their custom to meet, took the Bible from its humble shrine, and began turning over its leaves.

And why call ye me, Lord, Lord, and do not the things which I say?

He read the words over a second time, then a third, and sank deep in thought.

This is something like the way his thoughts went:

"What is he talking about? What had he been saying before? Let me look and see what he says, that I may begin to *do* it!"

He read all the chapter again and found it full of *tellings*. When he read it before, he had not thought of actually doing a single one of the things Jesus said. He had not seen himself as involved in any of the matters at hand.

"I see!" he exclaimed. "We must begin at once to *do* what he tells us, not just read about it!"

He ran to find his brother.

"I've got it!" he cried. "I've got it!"

"What?"

"What we're to do."

"What is it?"

"Just what he tells us."

"We were doing that," said Sandy, "when we prayed for him to tell us what to pray for."

"So we were! That's good."

"So are we supposed to pray for anything more?"

"We'll soon find out. But first we must look for something to do."

They began at once to search through the whole book of Matthew for things the Lord told them to do. And of all they found, the plainest and simplest for their young minds to grasp was: "Whosoever shall smite thee on thy right cheek, turn to him the other also."

This needed no explanation! It was as clear as the day to both of them. The very next morning the schoolmaster, who, though of a gentle disposition, was irritable, took Andrew for the offender in a certain breach of discipline, and gave him a smart box on the ear. As readily as if it had been instinctive, Andrew turned to him his other cheek.

An angry man is an evil interpreter of holy things, and Mr. Fordyce took the action for one of rudest mockery, and did not think of the higher master therein mocked, if indeed it had been a mockery: and struck the offender a yet harder blow. Andrew stood for a minute like one dazed, but the red on his face was not that of anger. Rather, he was perplexed as to whether he ought now to turn the former cheek again to the striker. Uncertain, he turned away and went back to his work.

Does one of my readers stop here to say, "Do you really mean to tell us we ought to take the words of the Bible literally as Andrew did?"

I answer, "When you have earned the right to understand, you will not need to ask me. To explain what the Lord means to one who is not obedient is the work of no man who truly knows his work."

It is only fair to say on behalf of the schoolmaster that, when he found he had been mistaken, he tried to make up to the boy for it—not by confessing himself wrong—who could expect that of only a schoolmaster?—but by being kinder to him than before. Through this effort the schoolmaster came to like him, and from time to time would attempt to teach the young lad things out of the usual way—such as how to make different kinds of verse.

After the passage of some time Andrew and Sandy had another quarrel. In the very midst of it, suddenly Andrew came to himself and cried, "Sandy! He says we're to agree!"

"Does he?"

"He says we're to love one another, and we can hardly do that if we don't agree." Then came a pause. "Perhaps you were right after all, Sandy," said Andrew.

"I was just going to say, now that I think about it, that perhaps I wasn't so much in the right as I thought I was."

"It can't matter much who was in the right when we were both wrong for quarreling," replied Andrew. "We must ask him to keep us from caring which one of us is in the right and make us both try to be right in our attitudes. For it's my job to take care of you."

"And mine to take care of you, Andrew."

"Look here, Sandy," said Andrew, "we must have another, and then there'll be four of us."

"How's that?"

"I wonder that we never noticed it before! He says, 'Where two or three are gathered together in my name, there am I in the midst of them.' It stands to reason that three must be better than two. First one must love him, and then two can love him better, because each one is helped by the other, and loves him the more that he loves the other one. And then comes the third, and there's more and more throwing of light, and there's the Lord himself in the midst of them. Three makes a better midst than two!"

Sandy could not quite follow his brother's reasoning, but he had his own way of understanding the matter.

"It's just like the story of Shadrach, Meshach, and Abednego," he told him. "There was three of them, and so he made four."

Here now was the nucleus of a church indeed—two stones laid on the one foundation stone. The idea of a third to join them was the very principle of growth. They would meet together and say: "O Father of Jesus Christ, help us to be good like Jesus." And then Jesus himself would become one of them and worship the Father with them.

The next thing, as a matter of course, was to look about for a third. "Dawtie!" cried both at once.

7 / The Childlike Three

Dawtie was the child of a cottar couple, who had an acre or two of the brothers' father's farm, and helped him with it. I never managed to learn her real name. *Dawtie* means *darling,* and is a common term of endearment—no doubt derived from the Gaelic *dalt,* signifying *a foster child.*

Dawtie was a dark haired, laughing little darling, with shy, merry manners, and the whitest of teeth, full of fun, but solemn in an instant. Her small feet were bare and black—except on Saturday nights and Sunday mornings—but full of expression, and perhaps really cleaner, from their familiarity with the sweet all-cleansing air, than such as hide all the day long in socks and shoes.

Dawtie's specialty was the love of animals.

She had an undoubting conviction that every creature with which she came in contact understood and loved her. She was the champion of the oppressed without knowing it. Like some boys, she had her pockets as well as her hands at the service of live things. But it was not a general interest in animals with her, but an individual love to the individual animal, whatever it might be, that presented itself to the love-power in her.

It may seem strange that there should be three such children together. But their fathers and mothers had for generations been poor—which was a great advantage, as may be seen in the world by him who has eyes to see, and heard in the parable of the rich man by him who has ears to hear. Also they were God-fearing, which was a far greater advantage and made them honorable. For they would have scorned things that most Christians think nothing of doing. Dawtie's father had a rare keen instinct for what is mean—not in others, but in himself—and when he saw meanness rear its head, he was abhorred by it. To shades and nuances of selfishness, which men of high repute and comfortable conscience would neither be surprised to find in their neighbors nor annoyed to find in themselves, he would give no quarter. Along with Andrew's father, in childhood and youth Dawtie's father had been under the influence of a simplehearted pastor, whom the wise and prudent laughed at as one who could not take care of himself. These scoffers were incapable of seeing that, like his Master, the pastor laid down his life that he might take it again. He left God to look after him that he might be free to look after God.

Little Dawtie had learned her catechism, but, thank God, had never thought about it or attempted to understand it—good negative preparation for becoming, in a few years more, able to understand the New Testament with the heart of a babe.

The brothers did not have to search long before they came upon her, where she sat on the ground at the door of her father's turf-built cottage, feeding a chicken with oatmeal paste.

"What are you doing, Dawtie?" they asked.

"I am trying to keep life in the chickie," she answered without looking up.

"What's the matter with it?"

"Nothing but the want o' a mither."

"Is its mother dead?"

"Na, she's alive enough, but she has too many bairns to help them all. Her wings winna cover them, and she drives this one away, and winna let it come near her."

"Such a cruel mother hen!"

"Na, she's no cruel. She only wants to make it come to me. She kenned I would take it. Ha, Flappy's a good mither. I ken her weel. She kens me, or she would have kept the puir thing, and done her best wi' her."

"There's somebody," said Andrew, "that wants to spread out

wings, like a great big hen, over *all* the bairns, you and me and all, Dawtie.''

''That's my mither!'' cried Dawtie, looking up and showing her white teeth.

''No, it's a man,'' said Sandy.

''It's my father, then!''

''No, not him either. Would you like to see him? Sandy and me's going to see him someday.''

''I'll go wi' ye.—But I must take my chickie along.''

She looked down where she had set the little bird on the ground; it had hobbled away and she could not see it.

''Eh!'' she cried, starting up, ''ye made me forget my chickie wi' yer questions! Its mither'll peck it!''

She darted off, leaving the tale of the Son of Man to go look for her chicken. But presently she returned with it in her hands.

''Noo, tell me more,'' she said, resuming her seat. ''What do they call him?''

''They call him the Father of Jesus Christ.''

''Oh, it's God ye mean! I ken him. I'll go wi' ye,'' she answered.

So the tiny church was increased by a whole half, and the fraction of a chicken—a type of the groaning creation waiting for sonship.

Whenever the three got together, either to talk or pray or read the New Testament, almost always there was some creature with them in the arms or hands of Dawtie—and, of course, the Lord himself was present. And if he was not there too, then, as the scripture says, are we Christians most miserable, for with him we see a glory beyond all that man could dream.

At other times they went on with the usual employments and games of children. But there was this difference between them and most grown Christians—when anything roused thought or question, they at once referred it to the words of Jesus, and having discovered his will, made haste to do it. Their faith was not theological, nor did they ever stop to consider whether their beliefs matched the tenets of the Shorter Catechism they had learned. Practicality was the only code between them: could something be *done*? If so, where was to be found the first opportunity to *do* it?

It naturally followed that, seeing he gives the spirit to them that obey him, they grew rapidly in the modes of their Master, learning to look at things as he looked at them, to think of them as he thought of them, to value what he valued, and despise what he despised—all in simplest order of divine development, in uttermost accord with highest reason, the whole turning on the primary and continuous effort to obey.

As they grew older the bond between the three increased. But with added years came no diminishing of the childlike simplicity of their faith. They rarely had any regular time of meeting, and when they came together one of them would read from the story and they would talk about any discoveries any had made concerning what Jesus would have them do. Then they would pray, but making no formal utterances, the three simply asked for what they needed. Here are some examples of their petitions:

"O Lord, I don't know anything to ask you for today, so just give us what we need, and what you want us to have, without our asking it."

"Lord, help me. I'm fighting a bad temper today, and you wouldn't have us like that."

"Lord, Dawtie's mother has a headache. Make her better, if you please." Dawtie rarely said a word, but sat and listened with her big eyes, generally stroking some creature in her lap. Surely the part of every superior is to help the life in the lower.

Once the question arose of what became of the creatures when they died.

They concluded that the sparrow which God cared for must be worth caring for, and they could not believe he had made it to last only such a little while as its life in this world. Thereupon the three agreed to ask the Lord that when they died, they might have again a certain dog, an ugly white mongrel they had been very fond of. All their days after this, they were, I believe, more or less consciously looking forward to the fulfillment of this petition. For their hope strengthened with the growth of their ideal, and when they had to give up any belief as a result of the maturity that comes with advancing years, it was always to take up a better in its place.

At length Sandy and Andrew, somewhere between their fourteenth and sixteenth years, I think, yielded the notion that the peddler was Jesus Christ. But they never ceased to believe that he was God's messenger, or that the Lord was with them always. They would not necessarily have insisted that he was walking about on the earth, but to the end of their days they cherished the uncertain hope that they might, even without knowing it, look upon the face of the Lord in some stranger passing in the street, or mingling in a crowd, or seated in a church. For they knew that all the shapes of man belong to the Lord, and that after he rose from the dead there were several occasions on which he did not at first look like himself to those to whom he appeared.

The childlike, the essential, the divine notion of serving—with their everyday will and being, the will of the living one, who lived for them that they might live, as once he had died for them that they might die—ripened in them to a Christianity that saw God everywhere, in everything, in every moment, saw that everything had to be done as God would have it done, and that nothing but injustice had to be forsaken to please him.

They were under no influence of what has been so well called *other-worldliness*. Their heads were not in the clouds, as it were, but very much joined to feet planted solidly on the earth. They saw this world as much God's as heaven might be, and saw that the world's work has to be done divinely, realizing that such doing is the beginning of the world to come. It was to them all one world, with God in it, all in all. Therefore the best work for the other world was the work of this world.

The common sense of the three young people rapidly developed, for there is no teacher like obedience, and no obstruction like its postponement. When in later years their mothers came at length to understand that obedience had been so long the foundation of their life, it explained to them many things that had seemed strange, and brought them to reproach themselves that they should have seemed strange.

It ought not to be overlooked that the whole thing was wrought in the children without directed influence of any kindred, neighbor, teacher, or pastor. They imitated no one. The galvanism of imitation is not the life of the spirit. The use of form where love does not exist is killing.

If anyone is desirous of spreading the truth, let him apply himself, like these children, to the doing of it. Not obeying the truth, he is doubly a liar who pretends to teach it. If he obeys it already, let him obey it more. It is life that awakens life. All form of persuasion is empty except in vital association with regnant obedience. Talking and not doing is dry rot.

One of Andrew's idiosyncrasies as a youngster was a great dislike to lumps in his porridge. One day his mother was less careful than usual in cooking it, and he made a wry face at the first spoonful.

"Andrew," said Sandy, "take no thought for what you eat."

It was a wrong interpretation but a righteous use of the word. Happy the soul that mistakes the letter only to get at the spirit!

Andrew's face smoothed itself, began to clear up, and broke at last into a sunny smile. He said nothing, but ate his full share of the porridge without a frown. This was practical religion, and if anyone judge it not worth telling, I count his philosophy worthless beside it. Such a doer knows more than such a reader will ever know, except he take precisely the same way to learn. The children of God do what he would have them do, and are taught of him.

There came a time when a report reached the pastor, now an old man of ripe heart and true insight, that certain children in his parish "played at the Lord's Supper." He was shocked, and went to see their parents.

They knew nothing of the matter. The three young people

were sought, and the pastor had a private interview with them.
He reappeared from it with a solemn, pale face and silent tongue.
The parents asked him the result of his inquiry. He answered that
he was not prepared to interfere. In the midst of his discussion
with them came the warning to his mind that there were such
things as necks and millstones.

The next Sunday he preached a sermon from the text, "Out
of the mouth of babes and sucklings thou has perfected praise."

The fathers and mothers made inquisition, and found no desire
on the part of their children to conceal what they had been doing.
Wisely or not, they forbade the observance. It cost Andrew much
thought whether he was justified in obeying them. In the end he
saw that right and wrong in itself was not concerned, and that the
Lord would have them obey their parents.

Such was the boyhood and youth of Andrew Ingram whom
Miss Fordyce now reproved for not setting the good example of
going to church.

It is necessary to tell so much of Andrew's previous history,
lest what remains to be told should perhaps be unintelligible or
seem incredible without it. A character like his cannot be formed
in a day; it must early begin to grow.

The bond thus bound between the children, altering in form
as they grew, was never severed. Nor was the lower creation ever
cut off from its share in the petitions of any one of them. Even
when circumstances forced them to cease being able to assemble
regularly together as a community of three, they each continued
to act on the same live principles.

Glad as their parents would have been to send them to college,
Andrew and Sandy had to leave school only to work on the farm.
But they carried their studies on from the point they had reached.
When they could not get further without help, they sought and
found it. For a year or two they went in the winter to an evening
school, but it took so much time to get there and back that they
found they could make more progress by working on their studies
at home. What help they sought went a long way, and what they
learned, they knew.

When the day's work was over and the evening meal past, it was their custom to go to the room their own hands had made convenient for study as well as sleep, and there resume the labor they had dropped the night before. Together they read Greek and mathematics, but Andrew worked mainly in literature, Sandy in mechanics. On Saturdays Sandy generally was busily involved making something with his hands—for his was an inventive mind—while Andrew either read to him or polished one of his own poems, which he hoped to send abroad, all the time asking Sandy's advice. On Sundays, they always read the Bible together for an hour or two.

The brothers were not a little amused with Miss Fordyce's patronage of Andrew. But they had now been too long endeavoring to bring into subjection the sense of personal importance to take offense at it.

Dawtie had gone into service as a domestic in a home in the next county, and they seldom saw her except when she came home for a few days at the end of a six-week term. She was a grown woman now, but the same loving child as before. She counted the brothers her superiors on the social scale, just as they counted the laird and his daughter their superiors. But whereas Alexa claimed the homage, Dawtie yielded where there was no thought of claiming it. The brothers regarded Dawtie as their sister. That she was poorer than they, only made them the more watchful over her, and if possible the more respectful to her. So she had a rich return for her care of the chickens and kittens and puppies.

8 / George and Andrew

George went home the very next day after the incident in the garden. The following week he sent Andrew a note, explaining that when he saw him he did not realize his obligation to him, and expressing the hope that he might call upon him the next time Andrew was in town.

Andrew recognized the condescension in George's words, to one in humble position who could not possibly even look with equality upon one in the same golden rank with himself. Perhaps the worst evil in the sense of social superiority is the vile fancy that it alters essential human relation. But Andrew was not one to dwell upon his rights. He thought it friendly of Mr. Crawford to ask him to call. Therefore, though he had little desire to make his acquaintance, being far stronger in courtesy than the man who invited him, Andrew took the first Saturday afternoon to go and see him.

Mr. Crawford the elder lived in some style, and his door was opened by a servant whose blatant adornment filled Andrew with friendly pity: no man would submit to be dressed like that, he judged, except from necessity. The reflection sprang from no foolish and degrading contempt for household service. It is true Andrew thought no labor so manly as that in the earth, out of which grows everything that makes the loveliness or use of nature. For by such labor he came in contact with the primaries of human life, and was God's fellow laborer, a helper in the work of the universe, knowing the ways of it and living in them. But not the less would he have cheerfully done any service that his own need or that of others might have required of him. The colors of a parrot, however, were not fit for a son of man, and hence his look of sympathy when the man opened the door to let him in. Andrew's regard was met only by a glance of plain contempt, as the lackey, moved by the same spirit as his Master, left him standing in the hall—to return presently to show him into the library—a room of mahogany, red morocco, and yellow calf, where George was seated. He rose and shook hands with him.

"I am glad to see you, Mr. Ingram," he said. "When I wrote I had but just learned that I was indebted to you for helping rescue me from the train."

"It is scarcely worth mentioning."

"You call it nothing to carry a man of my size over a mile of heather?"

"I had help," answered Andrew. "And but for the broken leg," he added with a laugh, "I could have carried you well enough alone."

Then came a pause, for George did not quite know what to do with the farmer fellow next. So the latter spoke again, showing not the least embarrassment.

"You have a grand library, Mr. Crawford. It must be wonderful to sit among so many books. It's just like a wine merchant's cellars—only here you can open and drink, and leave the bottles as full as before."

"A good simile, Mr. Ingram!" replied George. "You must come and dine with me and we'll open another sort of bottle."

"You must excuse me, sir. I have neither time nor interest for that sort of bottle."

"I understand you read a great deal?"

"Weather permitting," replied Andrew.

"I should have thought that if anything was independent of the weather, it must be reading."

"Not a farmer's reading. To him the weather is the word of God, telling him whether to work or read."

George was silent. He had never been accustomed to think of

the word of God as anything but the Bible.

"But you must read a great deal yourself," resumed Andrew, casting a glance round the room.

"The books are my father's," said George.

He did not mention that nearly all his own reading came from the modern fare offered in the library cart, except when he wanted some special information, for George prided himself on being "a practical man." He read his Bible occasionally to prepare for his class in Sunday school, and his Shakespeare when he was going to see a performance of one of the plays. He would make the best of both worlds by paying due attention to both. He was religious, but liberal.

His father was a banker, an elder of the church, well reputed in and beyond his circle. He gave to many charities, and largely to educational schemes. His religion was to hold by the traditions of the elders and to keep himself respectable in the eyes of money dealers. He went to church regularly, and always asked God's blessing on his food, as if it were a kind of general sauce. He never prayed that God would give him love for his neighbor or help him to be an honest man. He went through "devotions" every morning, no doubt. But only a nonentity like his God could care for such prayers as his. George rejected his father's theology as false in logic and cruel in character. George knew just enough of God to be guilty of neglecting him.

"I can get by with less reading when I am out all day, but then I have the 'book of knowledge fair,' " said Andrew, quoting Milton. "It does not take *all* one's attention to drive a straight furrow, or keep the harrow on the edge of the last turn."

"You don't mean you can read your Bible as you hold the plough!" said George.

"Oh no," answered Andrew with a smile. "It would hardly be possible to manage a book between the stilts of the plough. The Bible will keep till you get home; a little of it goes a long way. I was speaking of nature. Paul counted the book of creation enough to make the heathen answerable for not minding it. Never a breath of wind wakes suddenly, or a cloud moves overhead, or a drenching rainfall stops my work, but that they talk to me about God. And is not the very sunlight itself the same that came out of the body of Jesus at his transfiguration?"

"You seem to have some rather peculiar notions, Mr. Ingram."

"Perhaps. But for a man to have no ideas he counts as his very own is much the same as to have no ideas at all. For a person to adopt as his beliefs only and nothing more than what he has heard from others seems to me a hollow faith. A man cannot have the ideas of another man any more than he can have another man's soul, or another man's body. Ideas must be one's own or they cease to truly be *ideas* at all."

"That is dangerous doctrine."

"Perhaps we are not talking about the same thing. I mean by *ideas* what a man orders his life by."

"Your ideas may be wrong."

"The All-wise will be my judge."

"So much the worse if you are in the wrong."

"Having him as my judge is good whether I be in the right or the wrong. I want him as my judge all the more when I am wrong, for then I most keenly need his wisdom. Would I have my mistakes overlooked? Not at all! Shall he not do right? And will he not set me right? I can think of nothing so wonderful!"

"That is a most dangerous confidence."

"It would be if there were any other judge. But it will be neither the church nor the world that will sit on the great white throne. He who sits there will not ask, 'Did you go to church?' or 'Did you believe this or that?' but, *Did you do what I told you?*"

"And what will you say when he asks that, Mr. Ingram?"

"I will say, 'Lord, only you know.' "

The answer checked George a little, and he did not reply immediately. At length he asked, "Suppose he should say you did not, what would you answer then?"

"I would say, 'Lord, send me where I may learn.' "

"And if he should say, 'That is what I gave you life in the world for, and you have not done it. You may have no second chances!' What would you say then?"

"I should hold my peace and say nothing."

Again George thought for a moment, then tried a new tactic in his questioning.

"So you do what he tells you, then?"

"I try."

"Does he not say, 'Forsake not the assembling of yourselves together'?"

"No, sir, he does not."

"What!"

"Somebody says something like it in the epistle to the Hebrews."

"And isn't that the same?"

"The man who recorded Hebrews realized that all he wrote had to be understood in light of the life of the Messiah. Sir, it is the Lord's instructions and life I try to model my deeds and thoughts by, no one else's. Tell me, Mr. Crawford, what makes a gathering a church?"

"It would take me some time to arrange my ideas before I could answer you," replied George, uncertain to unexpectedly find himself on the other end of the questioning.

"Is it not the presence of Christ that makes an assembly a church?"

"I suppose that is true," said George hesitantly.

"Does he not say that where two or three are met in his name, there he is in the midst of them?"

"Well?"

"Then thus far will I justify myself to you, that, if I do not go to what you call *church,* I yet often make one of such a company met in his name."

"He does not limit the company to two or three."

"Assuredly not. But if I find I get more help and strength with a certain few, why should I go to a gathering of a multitude to get less? Will you draw another line of definition than the Master's? Why should it be more sacred to worship with five hundred or five thousand than with three? If he is in the midst of them, they cannot be wrongly gathered."

"It looks as if you thought yourselves better than everybody else."

"I consider myself better than no man. Besides, if it were such that we thought, then certainly he would not be one of the gathering."

"How are you to know that he is in the midst of you?"

"His presence cannot be proved; it can only be known. One thing for certain, if we are not keeping his commandments, he is not among us. But if he does meet us, it is not necessary to the joy of his presence that we should be able to prove that he is there. If a man has the company of the Lord, he will care little whether someone else does or does not believe that he has."

"Your way fosters division in the church."

"Did the Lord come to send peace on the earth? My way, as you call it, would indeed make division, but division between those who *call* themselves his, and those who *are* his. It would bring together those that love him. Company would merge with company that they might look on the Lord together. I don't believe that Jesus cares much for what is called the visible church. But he cares with his very Godhead for those who do as he tells them. They are his Father's friends. They are his elect by whom he will save the world. It is by those who obey, and by their obedience, that he will save those who do not obey, that is, will bring them to obey. It is one by one the world will pass to his side. There is no saving of the masses. If a thousand be converted at once, it is still every single lonely man that is converted."

"You would make a slow process of it."

"It is slow, yet faster than any other. All God's processes are slow. The works of God take time and cannot be rushed."

"How does that help one who has no time?"

Andrew thought for a moment, then said, "Let me attempt to answer you in this way: How many years has the world existed, do you imagine?"

"I don't know. Geologists say hundreds and hundreds of thousands, maybe millions."

"And how many is it since Christ lived?"

"Almost two thousand."

"Then we are but in the morning of Christianity! There is plenty of time. The day is before us."

"Dangerous doctrine for the sinner!"

"Why? Time is plentiful for his misery if he will not repent, plentiful for the mercy of God that would lead him to repentance. There is plenty of time for labor and hope, but none for indifference and delay. God *will* have his creatures good. They cannot escape him."

"Then a man may put off repentance as long as he pleases."

"Certainly he may—at least as long as he can—but it is a fearful thing to try issues with God."

"I can hardly say I understand you."

Andrew paused again. This time it was a little longer before he spoke, during which interval he offered up a silent prayer—both for the heart of his listener and for humility in his own spirit. At last he opened his mouth once more.

"Mr. Crawford," he said quietly, "you have questioned me in the way of kindly anxiety and reproof. Thus perhaps that has given me the right to question you. Tell me, do you think we are bound to do what our Lord requires?"

"Of course. How could any Christian man or woman do otherwise?"

"Yet it is possible for a man to say 'Lord, Lord' and still be cast out."

"And?"

"In other words, it is possible for one who seems a Christian, who calls him *Lord,* to be cast into the fire. It is one thing to say we are bound to do what the Lord tells us, and another to *do* what he tells us.''

"That I would grant.''

"He says, 'Seek ye *first* the kingdom of God and his righteousness.' Mr. Crawford, if you will forgive my boldness, are you seeking the kingdom of God *first,* or are you seeking money first?''

"We are sent into the world to make a living.''

"Sent into the world, we have to seek a living. We are not sent into the world to seek our living but to seek the kingdom and righteousness of God. And to seek a living is very different from seeking a fortune.''

"If you had a little wholesome ambition, Mr. Ingram,'' replied George in a bit of a huff, "you would be less given to judging your neighbors.''

Andrew held his peace, and George concluded that he had the best of the argument—which was all he wanted. Of the truth concerned he did not see enough to care about. Perceiving no good was to be done, Andrew was willing to appear defeated. He did not value any victory of discussion but only the victory of the truth, and George was not yet capable of being conquered by the truth.

"No,'' resumed George, with the regained composure of again holding the upper hand, "we must avoid judging others. There are certain things all respectable people have agreed to regard as right. He is a presumptuous man who refuses to regard them. Reflect on it, Mr. Ingram.''

A curious smile hovered about the lip of the ploughman. When things to say did not come to him, he did not go and try to fetch them, but held his tongue. Long before, he had learned that when one is required to meet an untruth, words are given him; when they are not, silence is best. A man who does not love the truth, but disputes for victory, is the swine before whom pearls must not be cast. Andrew's smile meant that it had been fruitless to attempt a meeting of the minds with George upon a subject so holy as obedience to the Master.

As he left the house a few minutes later, a carriage drove up, in which sat Mr. Crawford the elder, home from a meeting of the directors of his bank, at which a dividend had been agreed upon— to be paid from the capital in preparation for another issue of shares of stock.

Andrew walked home in silent conversation with himself. *How can it be,* he wondered, *that so many who would be terrified at the idea of not being Christians, and are horrified at any man who does not believe there is a God, are yet absolutely indifferent to what their Lord tells them to do if they would be his disciples?*

"Oh, God," he broke out in speechless prayer, "keep me from doing that very thing without knowing it. Be all in all to me, oh, my God, for in you I have everything! The world is mine because it is yours! I thank you, Lord, that you have shown me whence I came, to know to whom I belong, and to know who is my Father and makes me his heir! I am yours infinitely more than my own, and you are mine, as you are Christ's!"

Andrew was one of the inheritors of the earth. He knew his Father in the same way that Jesus Christ knows his Father. He was at home in the universe, neither lonely, nor out of doors, nor afraid.

9 / The Fall of the House of Crawford_____

Though having strived all his days to secure his life, in the end Mr. Crawford lost it—both in God's sense of loss and his own. As is the case with all forms of mammon—possession of it satisfies not, and only increases the hunger for more. Mr. Crawford, though a rich man by any standards, hungered so mightily after wealth that his dubious investments and schemes eventually whipped their tail around and ensnared him from behind—proving again that the closer a man is to gaining his millions, the closer also lurks his financial collapse.

He narrowly escaped being put in prison for defrauding the investors in his bank, died instead, and was put into God's prison to pay the uttermost farthing. But he had been, in the eyes of the world, such a good Christian that his fellow Christians mourned over his financial failure and his death, not over his dishonesty. For did they not know that if he could have just managed to recover his footing—even if it took more dishonesty to do it!— he would have repaid everything?

Only one injunction he obeyed—he provided for his own. More than all the widows who trusted his bank with their meager savings, only his widow was safe from want. And she, like a dutiful wife cut from the same cloth as her husband, took care that his righteous intention should be righteously carried out. Therefore, not a penny would she give to the paupers her husband's deceit had made.

The downfall of the house of cards took place a few months after George's return to its business. Not initiated to the mysteries of his father's transactions, and thus ignorant of what had long been threatening, it was a terrible blow to him. The bank was ruined, his name was disgraced: what was he to do? But George was a man of action. At home he could no longer hold up his head. He therefore at once looked toward America for his future.

He had often been to Potlurg after the end of his convalescence, and had been advancing in intimacy with Alexa. But once the news of the bank was out, he determined he would not show himself there again until he could appear as a man of decision—until he was on the point of departure. Under such circumstances she would be the more willing to believe his innocence of complicity in the deceptions that had led to his father's ruin. He would thus also manifest self-denial and avoid the charge of selfish motives with respect to Alexa; he could not face the suspicion of being a suitor with nothing to offer! George had always taken the grand role—that of superior, benefactor, bestower. He was powerful in condescension.

Therefore, it was not until the night before he sailed that he went once more to Potlurg.

Alexa received him with a shade of displeasure.

"I am going away," he said abruptly the moment they were seated. Her heart gave a painful throb in her throat, but she did not lose her self-possession.

"Where are you going?" she asked.

"To New York," he replied. "I have got a job there—in a not unimportant firm. *There* at least I will be taken for an honest man! But from your heaven I have fallen. That is the worst of it."

"No one falls from any heaven unless he has himself to blame," rejoined Alexa.

"Where have I been to blame? I was not in my father's confidence. I knew positively nothing of what was going on."

"Then why did you so suddenly stop coming to see me?"

"A man who is neither beggar nor thief is not willing to appear either."

"You would have come if you had trusted me," she said.

"You must pardon pride in a ruined man," he answered. "Now that I am leaving tomorrow, I do not feel the same dread of being misunderstood."

"If you knew yourself trustworthy, George, why did you not think me capable of trusting? It was not kind of you."

"But, Alexa—a man's own father!"

For a moment he showed signs of an emotion he had seldom had to repress. She suddenly realized his anxieties were genuine.

"I beg your pardon, George!" she cried. "I am being both stupid and selfish!—Are you really going to America?" Her voice trembled.

"I am—but to return, I hope, in a very different position."

"You would have me understand—?"

"That I shall then be able to hold up my head."

"Why should an innocent man ever do otherwise?"

"Because he cannot help seeing himself in other people's thoughts, and as they see him."

"If we are in the right, ought we to care what other people think of us?" asked Alexa.

"Perhaps not. But I would rather have them think of me as I choose, not as circumstances dictate."

"How?"

"By compelling their respect."

"You mean by making a fortune?"

"Yes."

"Then it will be the fortune they respect, not yourself, and you will be no more worthy in their eyes."

"Perhaps, but there will still be respect shown, in any case."

"But is such a respect worth having?"

"Not in itself."

"In what, then? Why lay yourself out and work so hard for it?"

"Even the real respect of such people would be worthless to

me, Alexa. I only want to bring them to their knees so they will know they misjudged me."

Even though Alexa seemed to take the right side of the argument, the disease of mammon was equally rooted in her, though in different form than the pure love of fortune that George now espoused as his goal. The truth was, Alexa prized social position so dearly that she did not relish his regarding it as a thing at the command of money. George could become as rich as any London financier, or any Jew or any American, but Alexa would never regard him as her equal! George worshiped money; Alexa worshiped birth and land.

The eyes of the soul have such keen but partial vision. Our own way of being wrong is all right in our own eyes. Our neighbor's way of being wrong, however, is offensive to all that is good in us. We are therefore kindly anxious to pull the mote out of his eye, never thinking of the big beam standing in the way of the operation. Jesus labored to show us that our immediate business is to be right in ourselves. Until we are, even our righteous indignation is waste.

While he spoke, George's eyes were on the ground. His grand resolve did not give his innocence strength to look in the face of the woman he thought he loved. He felt, without knowing why, that she was not satisfied with him. Of the paltriness of his ambition, he had no inward hint. The high resolves of a puny nature must be a laughter to the angels—the bad ones.

"If a man has no ambition," he resumed, feeling after her objection, "how can he possibly fulfill the end of his being? No sluggard ever made a permanent mark. How would the world advance but for the men who have to make their fortunes? If a man finds his father has not made money for him, what else is he to do but make it for himself? You would not have me be a clerk all my life! If I had but known how things were going to turn out, I should by this time have been well ahead!"

Alexa had nothing to answer. It all sounded very reasonable. Were not Scot boys everywhere taught that it was the business of life to rise? In whatever position they were in, was it not their part to get out of it—to a higher one?

She did not see any better than George that it is in the kingdom of heaven only that we are bound to rise. We are born into the world not to rise *in* the kingdom of Satan but to rise *out* of it. And the only way to rise in the kingdom of heaven is to do the work given us to do. Whatever be intended for us, this is the only way to do it. We have not to promote ourselves, but to do our work. It is the master of the feast who says, "Go up." If a man go up of himself, he will find he has mistaken the head of the table.

More talk followed, but neither cast any light. Neither saw the true question. George took his leave. Alexa said she would be glad to hear from him.

Alexa did not like the form of George's ambition—to gain money, and thereby compel the respect of persons he did not himself respect. But was she herself clear of the money disease? Would she have married a poor man? Would she not have been ashamed for George to know how she had supplied his needs while he lay in the house—that it was with the poor gains of her poultry yard that she fed him? Did it improve her moral position toward money that she regarded business with contempt—a rudiment of the time when nobles treated merchants as a cottager his bees?

George's position was a subordinate one in an investment house of large dealings in Wall Street.

Is not the church supposed to be made up of God's elect? And yet most of my readers will find it hard to believe that there should be three persons such as Andrew, Sandy, and Dawtie, so related, who agreed to ask of God neither riches nor love, but that he should take his own way with them, that the Father should work his will in them, and that he would teach them what he wanted of them, and help them to do it.

The church is God's elect, and yet you cannot believe in three holy children? Do you say, "Because they are represented as beginning to obey so young"?

"But if the young cannot obey," I answer, "then there can be no principle such as Jesus spoke of, but only an occasional and arbitrary exercise of spiritual power—in the perfecting of praise out of the mouth of babes and sucklings, or in the preference of them to the wise and prudent as the recipients of divine revelation. If he said it, I would further contend that what he spoke must be a principle of truth, not a mere spiritual accident."

Dawtie never said much, but tried to live her faith all the more. With heartiness she accepted what conclusions the brothers came to, so far as she understood them—and what was practical she understood as well as they, for she had in her heart the spirit of that Son of Man who chose a child to represent him and his Father. As to what they heard whenever they went to the parish church, their minds were so set on doing what they found in the gospel that it passed over them without even rousing their intellect, and so vanished without doing them any harm. Tuned to the truth by obedience, no falsehood they heard from the pulpit partisans of God could make a chord vibrate in response. Dawtie, indeed, heard nothing but the good that was mingled with the falsehood, and shone like a lantern through a thick fog.

She was little more than a child when, with sad hearts, her parents realized it was time for her to go out in service. Every six months she came home for a few days, and neither feared nor found any relation altered. At length, however, because of circumstances involving no fault of hers, she found herself without a job. Miss Fordyce heard of it, went to the cottage, and proposed to Dawtie's parents that the girl could help Meg, Alexa's servant, who was growing old and rather blind, until she could be replaced. Dawtie would thus be able to go on learning rather than idling at home, Alexa said.

Dawtie's mother was not a little amused at the idea of anyone idling in her house, not to say Dawtie, who would have found idleness more difficult than any amount of work. But she judged it right to accept the offer, if for no other reason than that Miss Fordyce might see what sort of girl Dawtie was.

Dawtie had hardly been at Potlurg a week before Meg began to complain that the girl did not leave work enough to keep the old servant warm. No doubt it gave her time for her book, but her eyes were not so good as they used to be, and she was apt to fall asleep over it and catch cold. But when her mistress proposed to send her away, old Meg would not hear of it. By this time Alexa herself had begun to take an interest in Dawtie, and so set her to do things Alexa had till then done herself. Before three months had passed, the girl was such a necessity in the house that to part with her seemed impossible. A place turned up about that time, and in order to keep Dawtie, Alexa at once offered her comparable wages, and so Dawtie became an integral portion of the laird's modest household.

The laird himself at length began to trust Dawtie as he had never trusted a servant before, for he even taught her to dust his precious books, which he had always done himself up till then, but lately had avoided, finding that not a few of them liberated asthma at the merest unclosing.

Dawtie was now a grown woman, bright, gentle, playful, with loving eyes and a constant overflow of tenderness upon any creature that could receive it. She had small but decided and regular features, whose prevailing expression was confidence—not in herself, for she was scarcely even conscious of herself even in the act of denying herself, but in the person upon whom her trusting eyes were turned. She was in the world to help—with no political economy beyond the idea that for help and nothing else did anyone exist. To be as the sun and the rain and the wind, as the flowers that lived for her and not for themselves, as the river that flowed, and the heather that bloomed lovely on the bare moor in the autumn, such was her notion of being.

That she had to take care of herself was a falsehood which never entered her brain. To do what she ought, and not do what she ought not, was enough on her part, and God would do the rest.

I will not say she mindfully reasoned in this fashion. To herself she was scarcely a conscious object at all.

Both bodily and spiritually she was in the finest health. If illness came, she would perhaps then discover a self with which she might have to fight—I cannot tell. But my impression is that she had so long done the true thing that illness would only develop unconscious victory, perfecting the devotion of her simple righteousness.

It is because we are selfish, with that worst selfishness which is incapable of recognizing itself, not to say its own loathsomeness, that we have to be made ill. The reason age and death overtake the saints themselves is that they may leave the last remnants of their selfishness. Suffering does not cause the vile thing in us—that was there all the time. Suffering comes to develop in us the knowledge of its presence that it may be war to the knife between us and it.

It was no wonder that Dawtie grew more and more of a favorite at Potlurg. She did not read much, but would learn by heart anything that pleased her, and then go saying or singing it to herself. She had the voice of a lark, and her song prevented many a search for her. Against her melodious voice, never the pride of the laird or the orderliness of the ex-schoolmaster ever put up the umbrella of rebuke. Her singing was so true, came so clear from the fountain of joy in her soul, and so plainly contained no desire to be heard or praised by others that it gave no annoyance. At the same time, such was the true sympathy of her nature that, although she had never suffered herself, upon hearing her sing "My Nannie's awa'!", you would have thought she was mourning over an absent lover from the very depths of her being. Her cleanliness was a heavenly purity, and so gently was all her work done that the very idea of fuss died in the presence of her labor. To the self-centered, such a person soon becomes a nobody, the more dependent they are upon her unfailing ministration; the less they think of her. But they have another way of regarding such in "the high countries." Hardly anyone knew her real name; she was known only by her pet name *Dawtie*.

Alexa wondered at times why she could not interest her in things her mistress gave her to read. She little knew how superior the girl's choice was to her own. Though Dawtie read little, she read well, and digested it thoroughly. Not knowing much of literature, what she liked was always of the best in its kind, and nothing without some best element could interest her at all. As from the first, Andrew continued to influence her reading. A word now and then with the books he lent or gave her was sufficient. That Andrew liked this or that was enough to make Dawtie set herself to find in it what Andrew liked, and it was thus she became acquainted with most of what she learned by heart.

Sandy had lately given up farming to pursue the development of certain inventions of his that had met with the approval of a man of means who, unable to make things himself, could yet understand a device. He took a liking to Sandy, and saw that there was use, and consequently money in his ideas, and thus wisely began investing his own money in Sandy's power to perfect them.

Consequently Sandy was mostly away from home, and when Dawtie went to see her parents, as she could much oftener now, Andrew and she generally met without a third. However many weeks might have passed, they always felt as if they had parted only the night before. There was neither shyness nor forwardness in Dawtie. Perhaps a livelier rose might tinge her sweet round cheek when she saw Andrew. Perhaps a brighter spark shone in the pupil of Andrew's eye. But they met as calmly as two prophets in the secret of the universe, neither anxious nor eager. The old relation between them was the more potent that it made so little outward show.

"Do you have anything for me, Andrew?" Dawtie would say, in the dialect which her sweet voice made so pleasant to those that loved her. Perhaps without immediate answer more than a smile, Andrew would generally turn into his room and reappear with what he had got ready for her to chew upon till they should meet again. Milton's sonnet, for instance, to the "virgin wise and pure," had long served her aspiration. Equally wise and pure, Dawtie could understand it as well as she for whom it was written. To see the delight she took in it would have been a joy to any loving student of humanity. It had cost her more effort to learn than almost any song, and perhaps therefore it was all the more precious. Andrew seldom gave her a book to learn from. In general he copied out in his own handwriting whatever poem or paragraph he thought fit for Dawtie.

There was a secret between them—a secret proclaimed on the housetops, a secret hidden, the most precious of pearls, in their hearts—that the earth is the Lord's and the fullness thereof. Before every man's eyes this secret silently shouts its truth, yet remains unseen and unheard by all but those with eyes to see and ears to hear. A secret it was indeed, yet the most life-giving truth in all the world—that the work done on the earth is the work of the Lord, whether the sowing of the field, the milking of the cow, the giving to the poor, the spending of wages, the reading of the

Bible; that God is all in all, and every throb of gladness is his gift; that their life came fresh every moment from his heart, that what was lacking to them would arrive the very moment he had got them ready for it.

They were God's little ones in God's world—nonetheless their own that they did not desire to swallow it or thrust his provision in their pockets. Among poverty-stricken Christians, consumed with care to keep a hold of the world and save their souls, they were as two children of the house. By living in the presence of the living one, they had themselves become his presence—dim lanterns through which his light shone steady.

He who obeys, shines.

11 / Sandy in America

Sandy had devised a machine, the value of which not even his patron could be convinced—that is, he could not see the prospect of its making money fast enough to constitute it a *good thing*. Sandy, however, regarded it as a discovery that would wonderfully uplift a certain downtrodden portion of the community and was determined not to give up on it—not primarily for the money to be made but by virtue of the good to be accomplished.

Having saved a little money on his own, Sandy therefore resolved to sail to the States, where insights into probabilities were fresher, to see if he could make his machine known and discover some means whereby it could be developed and put into use.

He was there a good many months, and when nearly a year had passed, Andrew received a letter from his brother in which he mentioned that he had come across Mr. Crawford, already of high repute in Wall Street. His countryman had been kind to him, Sandy said, and having learned his object in visiting America, and the approximate financial risk involved in bringing out his invention, had taken the thing into consideration.

But by almost the next mail came another letter to the effect that, having learned in more detail the nature of the business done by Mr. Crawford, he found himself unable to distinguish between it and gambling, or worse. Sandy said it seemed to him a vortex whose very emptiness drew money into it. He had therefore drawn back, and declined to put the thing in Crawford's hands.

Andrew gave the letter to Dawtie to read that she might see that Sandy remained a true man, even in the midst of his many business dealings. Andrew had never been anxious on the point, but was nevertheless very glad to see confirmation of the fact.

Dawtie took the letter with her to read at her leisure. Unable, however, to understand something Sandy said concerning Mr. Crawford's business, she asked a question or two of her mistress. Curious, Alexa questioned Dawtie and drew out of her that it had to do with a communication received of Andrew by his brother. She questioned further. Finding at length what was the subject of Sandy's letter, she asked to see it. Dawtie asked Andrew's permission, and then gave it to her.

Alexa was both distressed and indignant. Instantly she became George's partisan. Her distress diminished and her indignation increased as she reflected on the direction from which the unfavorable report reached her: the brothers were such peculiar men! What right had they to judge one so far above them! She recalled the strange things she had heard of their childhood. No doubt their judgments were formed on an overstrained and Quixotic idea of honesty! Besides, there had always been a strong socialistic tendency in them, which explained how Sandy could malign his benefactor! George was incapable of doing anything dishonorable. She would not trouble herself about it. Still, she would like to know how Andrew regarded the matter.

Therefore, at the first opportunity she asked him what he thought of Sandy's procedure. Andrew replied that he did not know much about business, but that the only safety must lie in having nothing to do with what was doubtful. Therefore, Sandy had done right.

Alexa said it hardly seemed right for him to condemn where he confessed ignorance.

Andrew replied, "If Mr. Crawford is wrong, he is condemned whether I know or say anything about it. I offer no judgment. If he is spotless in his business dealings, I will rejoice to learn of it, and my private doubts cannot hurt him. But Sandy must act by his own discernment in the matter, not by Mr. Crawford's confidence."

Alexa grew more distressed, for she began to recall things
George had said which at the time she had not liked, but which
she had succeeded in forgetting. But the judgment of such a man
as Sandy could settle nothing in her mind. Of humble origin and
childish simplicity, he could not see the thing as a man of experience must! At the same time, she thought, there *was* George's
father—whose reputation remained under a thick cloud. Breed
must go for something. It was the first time Alexa's thoughts had
turned into such a channel of doubt. She concluded that something
must have passed when they met to set the religious young farmer
against the banker's son. She would not utter George's name to
Andrew ever again!

She was right in thinking that George cherished a sincere
affection for her. It was one of the spurs that drove him too eagerly
after money. I doubt if any man starts with a developed love of
money for its own sake—except, indeed, he be born of generations of mammon worshipers.

George had gone into speculation with the object of retrieving
the position in which he had supposed himself born, and in the
hope of winning the hand of his cousin—thinking too much of
himself to offer what would not in the eyes of the world be worth
her acceptance. When he stepped on the inclined plane of dishonesty, he believed himself only engaging in "legitimate speculation." But he was at once affected by the atmosphere about
him. Wrapped in the breath of admiration and adulation surrounding men who cared for nothing but moneymaking, and constantly
under the softly persuasive influence of low morals and extravagant appreciation of cunning, he came by rapid degrees to think
less and less of right and wrong.

At first he called the doings of the place dishonest. Then he
called them sharp practice. Then he called them a little shady.
Then, close sailing. Then he said this or that transaction was
deuced clever. Then the man was more rogue than fool. Then he
laughed at the success of the vile trick. Then he touched the pitch,
and thinking all the time it was but with one finger, he was pres-

ently besmeared all over—as was natural, for he who will touch is already smeared.

While Alexa was fighting his battles with herself, George had thrown down his arms in the only battle worth fighting. When he wrote to her, which he did regularly, he said no more about business than that his prospects were encouraging. How much his reticence may have had to do with a sense of her disapproval, I cannot tell.

12 / Mother and Daughter

One lovely summer evening, with a small bundle in her hand, Dawtie rose to the top of a grassy knoll and looked down on her parents' turf cottage in the distance. The sun was setting behind her, and she looked as if she had stepped from it as she touched the ground on which she stood, rosy with the rosiness of the sun, but with a light in her countenance that came from a higher source, from the same nest as the sun himself.

She paused a moment, then ran down the hill, where she found her mother in the midst of making the porridge. Mother and daughter neither embraced nor kissed nor even shook hands, but their faces glowed with delight, and words of joy and warmest welcome flowed between them.

"Ye haena lost yer job, hae ye, hinny?" said the mother.

"No, mither, there's no fear o' that, as lang's the laird or Miss Lexy's at home. They treat me, I winna say like one o' themsel's, but as if they would hae liked me for one o' themsel's if it had pleased the Lord to send me their way instead o' yers. Ye canna think hoo good they are to me."

"Then what's brought ye today?"

"I jist asked for a day off o' the work. I wanted to see Andrew."

"Eh, lass! I'm feart for ye! Ye mustn't set yer heart sae high. Andrew's the best o' men, but a lass canna hae a man to hersel' jist cause he's the best man in the world."

"What do ye mean by that, Mither?" said Dawtie, looking a little scared. "Am I not to love Andrew, 'cause he's almost as good as the Lord wad hae him? Wad ye hae me hate him 'cause he's good? Hasna he taught me to love God? What can ye mean?"

"What I mean, Dawtie, is that ye maunna think because ye love him, ye must hae him as yer ain man. Ye maunna think ye canna live wi'oot Andrew."

"It's true, Mither, I dinna ken what I should do wi'oot him. Isna he aye shovin' the door o' the kingdom a wee wider all the time to let me see in the better? It's small wonder I love him! But as for wanting him as my ain man, as ye hae Father—I wad be ashamed o' mysel' to even think o' such a thing!"

"Weel, bairn. Ye was aye a wise lass, an' I maun trust ye. Only look to yer heart."

"As for not lovin' him—me that canna look at a blind kitten wi'oot lovin' it—I canna weel help lovin', Mither. God made me sae, and didna mean me not to love Andrew."

Silence followed, but the mother was brooding.

"Ye maun bethink ye, lass, hoo far he's above ye," she said at length. As the son of the farmer on whose land her husband was a cottar, Andrew seemed to her what the laird seemed to old John Ingram, and what the earl seemed to the laird, though the laird's family was ancient when the earl's had not yet been heard of. But Dawtie understood Andrew better than did her mother.

"You and me sees him far above, Mither, but Andrew himsel' never thinks o' such things. He's sae used to lookin' up, he's forgotten to look doon. He holds his land frae a higher one than the laird, or the earl himsel'."

The mother was silent. She was faithful and true, but fed on the dried fish of logic and system and Roman legalism. She could not follow the simplicities of her daughter's religion, who trusted neither in notions about him, nor even in what he had done, but in the live Christ himself whom she loved and obeyed.

"If Andrew wanted to marry me," Dawtie went on, jealous for the divine liberty of her teacher, "which never came into his head!—for his head's taken up wi' far grander things—it wouldna be because I was but a cottarlass that he would or wouldna do what he thoucht to be in the right. But tomorrow's the Sabbath, and we'll hae a walk together."

"I dinna altogether like those walks ye take upon the Sabbath day," said the mother.

"Jesus walked on the Sabbath the same as any other day, Mither."

"Weel, he kenned what he was aboot!"

"And sae do I, Mither. I ken his will."

"He had aye something on hand fit to be done on the Sabbath."

"And so hae I tomorrow, Mither. If I was to do anything not fit in this world, lookin' oot o' the eye he gae me, wi' the hands and feet he gae me, I wad jist deserve to be nippit oot at once, or sent into the ooter mirk [darkness]."

"There's many maun fare ill then, lass."

"I'm sayin' it only for mysel'. I ken none sae to blame as I would be mysel' if I did such things."

"Isna that makin' yersel' oot better than ither folk, lass?"

"If I said I thought anything worth doin' but the will o' God, I wad be a liar. If I say man or woman has naethin' other to do in this world or the next, I say it believin' every one o' them maun came to it at the last. Few sees it yet, but the time's comin' when everybody will be as sure of it as I am. What wonder is it that I say it, wi' Jesus tellin' me the same frae mornin' to night!"

"Lass, lass, I fear ye'll be goin' oot o' yer mind!"

"It'll be into the mind o' Christ, then, Mither. I dinna care for my ain mind. I hae none o' my ain, and will stick to his. If I dinna make his mine and stick to it, I'd be lost!—Noo, Mither, I'll set doon my things and run over to the hoose and let Andrew ken I'm here."

"As ye will, lass, ye're beyond me! I'll say naethin' against a willful woman, for ye've been aye a good dochter. I trust I hae risen to hope the Lord winna be disappointed in ye."

Dawtie left her, and soon found Andrew in the stable, suppering his horses. She told him she had something to talk to him about and asked if he would let her go with him on his walk the next day. Andrew was delighted to see her, consented readily to her request, and she was back home before her mother had taken the milk from the press.

In a few minutes her father appeared and welcomed her with a sober joy. As they sat eating their humble supper a few minutes later, he could not keep his eyes off her, she sat looking so well and nice and trim. He was a good-looking, work-worn man, his hands absolutely horny with labor. But inside many such horny husks are ripening beautiful kingdom hands when dear welcome Death will loose and let us go from the grave clothes of the body that bind some of us even hand and foot. Rugged father and withered mother were beautiful in the eyes of Dawtie, and she and God saw them better than any other.

Good, endless good, was on the way to them all! It was so pleasant to be waiting for the best of all good things.

13 / Andrew and Dawtie's Walk_____

Dawtie slept in peace and happy dreams till the next morning, when she was up almost with the sun and out in his low clear light. The sun was strong again. The red labor and weariness from the night before were gone from his shining face.

Everything about her, thought Dawtie, seemed to know God, or at least to have had a moment's gaze upon him. How else could everything look so content, hopeful, and happy! It is the man who will not fall in with the Father's bliss to whom the world seems soulless and dull. Dawtie was at peace because she desired nothing but what she knew he was pleased to give her. Even had she cherished for Andrew the kind of love her mother feared, her Lord's will would have been her comfort and strength.

If anyone say, "Then she could not know what true love between a man and woman is," I answer, "That person does not know what the better love is that lifts the earthly object of their love into the serene air where can only thrive our love for Another. Only when we love him in the higher regions of our being will we likewise know how to love our fellows in that rarefied air of the spirit where only true love exists."

The scent of the sweetpeas growing against the turf wall entered Dawtie's soul like a breath from the fields of heaven, where the children made merry with the angels, the merriest of playfellows, and the winds and waters, and all the living things, and all the things half alive, all the flowers and all the creatures, were at their sportive call; where the little ones had babies to play with, and did not hurt them, and where dolls were neither loved nor

missed, being never even thought of. Such were the girl's imag-
inings as her thoughts went straying, inventing, discovering. She
did not fear that the Father would be angry with her for being his
child and playing at creation. Who indeed but one that in a loving
heart can *make* can rightly love the making of the Maker!

When they had their breakfast, and the old people were ready
for church—where they would listen a little, sleep a little, sing
heartily, and hear very little to wake hunger, joy, or aspiration—
Dawtie put a piece of oatcake in her pocket and went to join
Andrew where they had arranged to meet. She found him waiting,
sprawled out full length in a bush of heather, reading a book of
Henry Vaughan's, and drawing from it "bright shoots of ever-
lastingness" for his Sabbath-day's delight.

He read one or two of the poems to Dawtie, who was pleased
but not astonished. She was rarely astonished at anything. She
had nothing in her to make anything beautiful by contrast. Her
mind was of beauty itself, and anything beautiful was to her but
in the order and law of things—what was to be expected. Nothing
struck her because of its rarity. The rare was at home in her
country, and she was at home with it. When, for instance, Andrew
read, "Father of lights, what sunny seeds," she took it up at once
and understood it, felt that the good man had said the thing that
was to be said, and loved him for it. She was not surprised to
hear that the prayer was more than two hundred years old. Were
there not millions of years in front? Why should it be wonderful
that a few years behind men should have thought and felt as she
did, and had been able to say it as she never could? Had she not
always loved the little cocks, and watched them learning to crow?

"But, Andrew," she said at length, after he was through reading to her, "I want to tell you something that's troubling me. After
that, you can teach me what you like about the poem."

"Tell on, Dawtie," responded Andrew.

"One night, about a fortnight ago," she began, "I couldn't
sleep. I drove all the sheep I could gather in my brain over one
stile after another, but the sleep stuck to the wool of them, and

everyone took it away with him. I wouldn't have worried about it, but that I had to be up early and was feared I might sleep in.

"So I got up and thought to sweep and dust the hall and the stairs. Then if, when I lay down again, I should sleep too long, there would be a part of the next day's work done. You know, Andrew, what the house is like. At the top of the stair that begins directly where you enter the house, there is a big irregular place, bigger than the floor of your barn, laid with flagstone. It is just as if all the different parts of the house had been built at different times round about it, and then it was itself roofed in as an after-thought. That's what we call the hall. The spare room opens on the left at the top of the stair, and to the right, across the hall, beyond the swell of the short thick tower where you see the half of outside, is the door of the laird's study. Its walls are covered all round with books, some of them, mistress says, worth their weight in gold, they are so scarce. But the master trusts me to dust them. He used to do it himself, but now that he is getting old he does not like the trouble, and it makes him asthmatic. He says books need more dusting than anything else, but are in more danger of being hurt by it, and it makes him nervous to see me touch them. I have known him to stand an hour watching me while I dusted, looking all the time as if he had just taken a dose of medicine. So I often do a few books at a time, as I can, when he is not in the way to be worried with it. But he always knows where I have been with my duster and long-haired brush. And now it came across my mind as I lay there that I had better dust some of his books first of all, as it was a good chance to do so since he would be sound asleep. So I lighted my lamp, went straight to the study, and began where I last left off.

"As I was dusting, one of the books I came to looked so new and different from the rest that I opened it to see what it was like inside. It was full of pictures of mugs, and gold and silver jugs and cups—some of them plain and some colored. And one of the colored ones was so beautiful that I stood and looked at it. It was a gold cup, I suppose, for it was yellow, and all round the edge and on the sides, it was set with stones, like the stones in mistress's rings, only much bigger. They were blue and red and green and yellow, and more colors than I can remember. The book said it was made by somebody, but I forgot his name. It was a long name. The first part of it began with a *B*, and the second with a *C*, I remember that much. It was like *Benjamin,* but that wasn't it. I put it back in its place, thinking I would ask the master whether there really were such beautiful things, and then took down the next book.

"Now whether the next book I began to dust had been passed over between two times of dusting, I don't know, but it was so dusty that before I would go on I had to give the duster a shake, and the wind from doing so blew the lamp out. I took it up to go to the kitchen and light it again when all of a sudden I saw a light under the door of a wardrobe that was always locked, and where the master said he kept his most precious books.

"How strange!" I thought, *"a light inside a locked cupboard!* Then I remembered how in one place where I had been, in a room over the stable, there was a press whose door had no fastening except a bolt on the inside. That set me to thinking, and some terrible things came to me that made me remember it. So now I said to myself, 'There's someone in there, after the master's books! It was not a likely thing, that a thief could have gotten into the house, but the night is the time for fancies, you know, and in the dark you don't know what is likely and what is not. But one thing was clear to me, however—I ought to find out what the light meant. Fearful things darted one after the other through my head as I went to the door; but there was one thing I dared not do, and that was to leave it unopened and the light unexplained.

"So I opened it as softly as I could, in terror lest the thief should hear my heart beating. When I could peep in, what do you think I saw? I could not believe my eyes! There was a great big room! I rubbed my eyes and stared, then rubbed them again and looked—thinking to rub it away. But there it was, a big, odd-shaped room, part of it with round sides. And in the middle of the room was a table, and on the table a lamp, burning as I had never seen a lamp burn, and there sat the master at the table with his back to me.

"I was so astonished that I forgot I had no business there and ought to go away. But I just stood there, like a lost idiot. The laird was holding up to the light, between his two hands, the very cup I had been looking at in the book, the stones of it flashing all the colors of the rainbow! I should think the whole thing a dream if I did not *know* it was not. I do not believe I made any noise, for I could not move, but he started up with a cry to God to preserve him, set the cup on the table, threw something over it, caught up a wicked-looking knife, and turned around. His face was like that of a corpse, and I could see him tremble. I stood steady, it was no time then to turn away! I supposed he expected to see a robber, and would be glad when he discovered it was only me. But when he did, his fear changed to anger, and he came at me. His eyes were flaming, and he looked as if he would kill me. I was not frightened—poor old man, I was able for him any day—but I was afraid of hurting him. So I closed the door quickly and went softly to my own room, where I stood a long time in the dark, listening. But I heard nothing more. Andrew, what am I to do?"

"I don't know that you have to do anything. But there is one thing you should not do—that is, tell anybody what you have seen."

"I had to tell because I did not know what to do."

"The whole thing is no fault of yours. You acted to the best of your knowledge, and could not help what came of it. Perhaps nothing more will come. Leave the thing alone, and if he says anything, tell him exactly how it happened."

"But I don't think you see what it is that troubles me. I am afraid my master is a miser! The mistress and he take their meals in the kitchen like poor people. The room next to the study must be the dining room of the house—and though my eyes were fixed on the flashing cup, I could not help seeing that it was full of strange and beautiful things. Among them were pieces of fine furniture and paintings of knights when they fought on their horses' backs. Before people had money to hoard, they must have stored other things."

"Suppose he is a miser," said Andrew, "what could you do? How are you to help it?"

"That's what I want to know. I love my master, and there must be a way to help him. It was a terrible thing to see—him in the middle of the night, gazing at that cup as if he had found the most precious thing that can have existed on the earth. Poor man! He looked at the cup as you might a precious book. His soul was at it, feasting upon it!"

"And you love your master?"

"Yes, of course."

"Why do you love him, Dawtie?" asked Andrew.

"Because I'm set to love him. Besides, we're told to love our enemies—so surely we're to love our friends. And he has always been a friend to me. He never said a harsh word to me, even when I was handling his books. He trusts me with them. I can't help loving him, Andrew!"

"There's no doubt about it, Dawtie, you've got to love him. And you do love him!"

"But there's more than that, Andrew. To hear the laird talk, you would think he cared more for the Bible than for the whole world—not to say gold cups! The way he talks of the merits of the Savior, you would think he loved him with all his heart. But I cannot get it out of my mind, ever since I saw that look on his face, that he *loves* that cup—that it's his graven image—his idol! Why else should he get up in the middle of the night to—to—to—well, it was just like worshiping it!"

"You're afraid, then, that he's a hypocrite too?"

"I daren't think that—it's only for fear that I should stop loving him—and for me to do that would be just as bad."

"As bad as what, Dawtie?"

"I don't always know what I'm going to say," answered Dawtie, a little embarrassed, "and then when I've said it, I have to look and see what it means. But isn't it as bad not to love a human being as it is to love a thing?"

"Perhaps worse," said Andrew.

"Something must be done," she went on. "He can't be left like that. But if he has any love for his Master, how is it that the love of the Master does not cast out the love of mammon? I can't understand it!"

"That is a hard question. But a cure may be going on, and for some it takes a long time, even years to work it out."

"What if it shouldn't be begun yet!"

"That would be terrible!"

"Then what am I to do, Andrew? You always say we must *do* something. You say there is no faith but that which *does* something."

"The apostle James said so, a few years before I was born, Dawtie."

"Don't make fun of me—please, Andrew! I like it, but today I don't think I can bear it, my head is so full of the poor old laird."

"Make fun of you, Dawtie! Never! But I don't know how to answer you."

"Well then, what *am* I to do?" persisted Dawtie.

"Wait until you do know what to do. When you don't know what to do, don't do anything—and only keep asking the Thinker for wisdom. And until you know, don't let the laird see that you know."

"You would have me hide my knowledge from him! Is that not deceitful, Andrew?"

"Deceit is in the heart, Dawtie, and your heart is pure. I would only have you keep it from the laird for his sake until you see how the Master would deal between you and him. We would have him convicted of the spirit, not stumbled by ourselves. When the time comes to make the fact known, you will be shown."

With this answer Dawtie was content, and they turned to go home.

14 / The Picture of the Cup

The old laird had a noteworthy mental fabric. Believing himself a true lover of literature, especially of poetry, he would lecture for ten minutes on the right mode of reading a verse in Milton or Dante, but as to meaning would pin his faith to the majority of the commentators. He was discriminative to a degree altogether admirable as to the rightness or wrongness of a proposition with regard to conduct, never questioning within his soul whether there was any injunction upon himself to live by said propositions. He owed his respectability to the hereditary accident of good impulses without any corresponding effort of the will.

He was almost as orthodox as Paul before his conversion, lacking only the heart and courage to persecute. Whatever the eternal wisdom saw in him, the thing most present to his own consciousness was the love of rare historic relics. And this love was so mingled in warp and woof that he did not know whether a thing was more precious to him for its rarity, its monetary value, or its historic-reliquary interest.

Throughout all the years he was a schoolmaster, he saved every possible halfpenny to buy books, not because of their worth or human interest, but because of their literary interest or the scarcity of the particular book or edition. During his holidays he would go about questing for the prey that his soul loved, hunting after precious things. But not even the precious things of the everlasting hills would be precious to him until they had received the stamp of curiosity. His life consisted in a continual search for something new that was known as known of old.

It had hardly yet occurred to him that he must one day leave his things and exist without them, no longer to brood over them, take them in his hands, turn, and stroke, and admire them. Yet, strange to say, he would at times anxiously seek to satisfy himself that he was safe for a better world, as he *called* it—to feel certain, that is, that his faith was of the sort he supposed intended by Paul. Not that he himself had actually gathered anything from the writings of the apostle. All his notions came from the traditions of his church concerning the teaching of the apostle.

He was anxious, I say, as to his safety for the world to come. And yet, while his dearest joy lay treasured in that hidden room, he never thought of the hour when he must leave it all and go houseless and pocketless, empty-handed if not armless, in the wide, closetless space, hearing ever in the winds and the rain and the sound of the sea waves the one question: "Whose shall those things be which thou hast provided?" Like the rich man to whom God said the words, the laird had gathered much goods for many years—hundreds and hundreds of things, every one of which he knew, and every one of which he loved. A new scratch on the bright steel of one of his suits of armor was a scratch on his heart. The moth and rust troubled him sorely, for he could not keep them away, and where his treasure was, there was his heart, devoured by the same moth, consumed by the same rust.

His possessions thus caused him much mental suffering. He was more exposed to misery than the miser of gold, for the hoarded coin of the latter may indeed be stolen, but he fears neither moth nor rust nor scratch nor decay. The laird cherished his things as no mother her little ones. Nearly sixty years he had been gathering them, and their money-worth was great. But he had no idea of its amount, for he could not have endured the exposure and handling of them, which an evaluation must involve.

His love for his books had somewhat declined in the growth of his love for things, and now by degrees not very slow, his love of his things was graduating itself after what he supposed their monetary worth. His soul not only clave to the dust, but was going deeper and deeper in the dust as it wallowed. All day long he was living in the past and growing old in it—it is one thing to grow old in the past, and quite another to grow old in the present! As he took his walk about his farms, or sat at his meals, or held a mild, souless conversation with his daughter, his heart was growing old, not healthily in the present, which is to ripen, but unwholesomely in the past, which is to consume with a dry rot.

While he read the Bible at prayers, trying hard to banish worldly things from his mind, his thoughts were not in the story or the discussion he read, but hovering, like a bird over its nest, about the darlings of his heart. Yea, even while he prayed, his soul, instead of casting off the clay of the world, was loaded and dragged down with all the still-moldering, slow-changing things that lined the walls and filled the drawers and cabinets of his treasure chamber. It was a place not even his daughter knew the existence of, for before she had ever entered the house, he had taken with him a stonemason from the town and built up the entrance to it from the hall. Ever afterward he kept the other door of it that opened from his study carefully locked, leaving it to be regarded as the door of a closet.

It was as terrible as Dawtie felt it, that a live human soul should thus haunt the sepulchre of the past, and love the lifeless, turning a room hitherto devoted to hospitality and mirthful inter-action into the temple of his selfish idolatry. Surely, if left to himself, the ghost that loved it would haunt the place. But just as surely such could not be permitted, for it might postpone a thousand years his discovery of the emptiness of a universe of such treasures. Now he was moldering into the world of spirits in the heart of an avalanche of the dust of ages, dust material from his hoards, dust moral and spiritual from his withering soul itself.

The day after his discovery by Dawtie he was ill, which, common as is illness to humanity, was strange in his case, for he was seldom sick. He was unable to leave his bed. But he never said a word to his daughter, who alone waited on him, as to what had happened during the night. He had passed the rest of the time

sleepless and without the possibility of a dream to fall back on.
Yet when morning came he was in great doubt whether what he
had seen—namely, the face of Dawtie peeping in at the door—
was a reality or merely a vision of the night. For when he opened
the door that she had closed, all was dark, and not the slightest
sound reached his quick ear from the swift foot of her retreat. He
turned the key twice, and pushed two bolts, eager to regard the
vision as a providential rebuke of his carelessness in leaving the
door on the latch—for the first time, he imagined. Then he tottered
back to his chair, and sank on it in a cold sweat. For, although
the confidence grew that what he had seen was but "a false creation proceeding from the heat-oppressed brain," it was far from
comfortable to feel that he could no longer depend upon his brain
to tell him only the thing that was true. What if he were going
out of his mind, on the way to encounter a succession of visions—
without reality, but possessed of its power! What if they should
be such whose terror would compel him to disclose what most he
desired to keep covered? How fearful to be no more his own
master, but at the beck and call of a disordered brain.

It would be better if it had in fact been Dawtie, and that she
had seen in his hands Benvenuto Cellini's chalice made for Pope
Clement the seventh to drink therefrom the holy wine—worth
thousands of pounds! Perhaps she had seen it! No, surely she had
not! He must be careful not to make her suspicious. He would
watch her and say nothing.

But conscious of no wrong and full of love to the old man,
Dawtie showed an untroubled face when next she met him, and
he made up his mind that he would rather have her ignorant. From
that time on, naturally though childishly, he was even friendlier
to her than before: it was so great a relief to find that he had
nothing to fear from her!

The next time Dawtie was dusting the books, she felt strongly
drawn to look again at the picture of the cup. It now seemed to
hold in it a human life!

She took down the book and began where she stood to read

what it said about the chalice, referring as she read from letter-press to drawing. It was taken from an illumination in a missal, where the cup was known to have been copied, and it rendered the description in the letterpress unnecessary except in regard to the stones and designs on the hidden side. She quickly learned the names of the gems that she might see how many were in the high priest's breastplate and the gates of the new Jerusalem. She then proceeded to the history of the chalice. She read that as the years passed it had come into the possession of Cardinal York, the brother of Charles Edward Stuart, and had been entrusted by him to his sister-in-law, the Duchess of Albany, from whose house it disappeared, some said stolen, others said sold. It came next to the historic surface in the possession of a certain earl whose love of curiosities was well known. But from his collection again it vanished, this time beyond a doubt stolen, and probably years before it was missed.

A new train of thought was presently in motion in the mind of the girl: *The beautiful cup was stolen! It was not where it ought to be . . . it was not at home. It was a captive, a slave!*

She lowered the book, half closed, with a finger between the leaves, and stood thinking. She did not for a moment believe her master had stolen it, though the fear did flash through her mind. It had been stolen and sold, and he had at length bought it from someone whose possession of it was in no way suspicious—at least thus she reasoned. But he must know now that it had been stolen, for here with the cup was the book which said so! That would not be so serious if the rightful owner were not known. But he *was* known, and the thing ought to be his.

The laird might not be legally bound, she was not sure, to restore the cup at his own loss, for when he bought it he was not aware that it was stolen. But ethically he was surely bound to restore it at the price he had paid for it if the former owner would pay it. To make such restoration was but the barest justice, mere righteousness! No theft could make the owner not the rightful owner, even though other claims upon the thing might come in.

One ought not to be enriched by another's misfortune.

Dawtie was sure that a noble of the kingdom of heaven would not wait for the money, but would with delight send the cup where it ought to have been all the time. She knew better, however, than to expect such magnificence from the poor wizened soul of her master—a man who knew all about everything, and whom yet she could not but fear to *be* nothing. As Dawtie had learned to understand life, the laird did not yet exist. But he well knew right from wrong; therefore the discovery she had just made affected her duty toward him. It might be impossible to make an impression on the miserliness of a miser, but upon the honesty in a miser it might be possible. The goblet was not his!

But the love of things dulls the conscience, and he might not be able, having bought and paid for it, to see that the thing was not therefore *his*. He might defend himself from seeing it.

To Dawtie this made the horror of his condition all the darker. She was one of God's babes, who cannot help seeing the true state of things. Logic was to her but the smoke that rose from the burning truth. She saw what is altogether above and beyond reasoning and analysis: the right thing, the truth, whose lowest servant—the hewer of its wood, not the drawer of its water, the merest scullion and sweeper away of lies from the pavement of its courts—is logic.

With a sigh she woke to the knowledge that she was not doing her work. Rousing herself, she was about to put the book back on its shelf. But her finger was still in the place, and she thought she would have one more glance at the picture. To her dismay she saw that she had made a mark on the plate, and at once the enormity of making a dirty mark on a book her master had made her well aware.

She was in great distress. What was to be done?

She did not once think of putting the book away, saying nothing, and try to forget about it. If her master did not know, to reason that he would never know if she held her peace would have been a pressing and imperative argument for informing him at once. She had done him an injury, and the injury to his book must be confessed. There was nothing else to do.

"If only I'd been more careful!" she said to herself.

But then almost immediately it flashed upon her that perhaps the thing had been no accident at all, but that here was the open door for the doing of what was required of her with regard to the cup. She was bound to confess the wrong she had done, and that would lead into the disclosure of what she knew, making it comparatively easy to use some remonstrance with the laird, whom in her mind's eye she saw like a beggar man tottering down a steep road to a sudden precipice. Her duty was now so plain that she felt not even a desire to consult Andrew. She was not one to ask an opinion for the sake of mere talking about it. She went to Andrew only when she wanted light to do the right thing. When the light was around her, she knew well enough how to walk, and troubled no one.

At once she laid down the book and duster and went to find the laird. But he had slipped away to the town to have a rummage in a certain little shop in a back street, which he had not rummaged through for a long enough time, he thought, to have let something come in. It was no relief to Dawtie—the thing would be all the day in front of her instead of behind her! It burned within her, not like a sin, but like what it was—a confession unconfessed. Little wrong as she had done, Dawtie was yet familiar with the lovely potency of confession to annihilate the wrong. She knew it was the turning from the wrong that killed it, that confession gave the *coup de grace* to offense. Still, she dreaded not a little the displeasure of her master, and yet she dreaded more his distress.

She prepared the laird's supper with a strange mingling of hope and anxiety. She feared having to go to bed without telling him. But he came at last, almost merry, with a brown paper parcel under his arm, which he was very careful of. Poor man, he little knew there waited him at that moment a demand from the eternal justice—almost as terrible as "this night they require thy soul of thee!" The torture of the moral rack was ready for him at the hands of his innocent housemaid! In no way can one torture another more than by waking conscience against love, passion, or pride.

He laid his little parcel carefully on the supper table, said a rather shorter grace than usual, began to eat his porridge, praised it as very good, spoke of his journey and whom he had seen, and was more talkative than was his custom. He informed Alexa, almost with jubilation, that he had at length found an old book he had long been on the watch for—a book in ancient broad Scots that treated the laws of verse in a full, even exhaustive manner. He pulled it from his pocket.

"It is worth at least ten times what I gave for it!" he said.

Then came devotions. The old man read how David deceived the Philistines, telling them a falsehood as to his raids. He read the narrative with a solemnity of tone that would have graced the most righteous action: was it not the deed of a man according to God's own heart? How could it be other than right? A quibbler over insignificant ethical points ten times a week, he made no question of the righteousness of David's wickedness!

Then he prayed, giving thanks for the mercy that had surrounded them all the day, shielding them from the danger and death which lurked for them in every corner. Dawtie could not help wondering what he would say when death did get him. Would he thank God then? And would he see, when she spoke to him, that God wanted to deliver him from a worse danger than any out-of-doors? Would he see that it was from much mercy he was made more uncomfortable than perhaps ever in his life before?

At length his offering was completed—how far accepted, who can tell? He was God's, and he who gave him being would be his father to the full possibility of God. They rose from their knees. The laird took up his parcel and book. His daughter went with him.

15 / Dawtie and the Laird

As soon as Dawtie heard her mistress's door close, she followed her master to the study, and arrived just as the door of the hidden room was shut behind him.

There was not a moment to be lost!

She went straight to it and knocked rather loudly. No answer came. She knocked again. Still there was no answer. She knocked a third time; and after a little fumbling with the lock, the door opened a chink, and a ghastly face, covered with the dew drops of terror, peeped through.

She was standing back a little, and the eyes did not at once find the object they sought. Then suddenly they lighted on her, and the laird shook from head to foot.

"What is it, Dawtie?" he faltered out in a broken voice.

"Please, sir," answered Dawtie. "I have something to confess. Would you listen to me?"

"No, no, Dawtie! I am sure you have nothing to confess!" returned the old man, eager to send her away and prevent her from seeing the importance of the room whose entrance she had discovered. Finding she did not move, he went on. "Or," he said, "if you have done anything that you ought not to have done, confess it to God. It is to him you must confess, not to a poor mortal like me. For my part, if it lies with me, I forgive you, and that is the end of it. Go to bed, Dawtie."

"Please, sir, I can't. If you won't hear me out, I'll sit down at the door of this room and sit till—"

"What room, Dawtie? Do you call this a room? It's only a

wee bit closet where I say my prayers before I go to bed.''

But as he spoke, his blood ran cold within him, for he had uttered a deliberate lie—two lies in one breath: the bit closet was the largest room in the house, and he had never prayed a prayer in it since the first day he entered it! He was overcome with immediate guilt for what he had done, for he had always cherished the idea that he was one who would not lie to save his life. Worst of all, now that he had lied, he must hold to the lie! He dared not confess it! He stood trembling.

"I'll wait, sir," said Dawtie, distressed at his visible suffering, and more distressed that a man could lie who never forgot his prayers. Alas, he was further down the wrong road than she had supposed!

Ashamed for his sake, and also for her own, to look him in the face—for he imagined that she believed him, while she knew that he lied—she turned her back on him. He caught at his advantage, glided out of the closet door, and closed it behind him. When Dawtie again turned, she saw him in her power.

The moment of her trial was come. She had to speak now for life or death. But remembering the Lord's words to his disciples to take no care of how they should speak, she began by simply laying down the thing that was in her hand.

"Sir," she said, "I am very sorry, but this morning I made a dirty mark in one of your books."

Her words alarmed him a little, making him forget for the moment his more important fears. But he took care to be gentle with her; it would not do to offend her, for was she not aware that where they stood was a door by which he went in and out?

"You make me uneasy, Dawtie," he responded. "What book was it? Let me see it."

"I will, sir."

She turned to take it down, but the laird followed her, saying, "Just point it out to me, Dawtie. I will get it."

She did so. It opened to the very page.

"There is the mark," she indicated. "I am sorry something terrible."

"So am I," returned the laird. "But," he added, willing that she should feel his clemency, and knowing that the book was not a rare one, "it is still a book, and you will be more careful another time. For you must remember, Dawtie, that you don't come into this room to read the books but to dust them. I hope you can now go to bed with an easy mind."

Dawtie was so touched by the kindness and forbearance of her master that the tears rose in her eyes, and she felt strengthened for her task. What would she not have encountered for his deliverance!

"Please, sir," she said, "let me show you a thing perhaps you never happened to read."

She took the book from his hand—he was too much astonished to retain it—and turned over the page to the plate with the engraving and showed him the passage which stated that the cup had disappeared from the possession of its owner and had certainly been stolen.

Finding he said not a word, she ventured to lift her eyes to his, and saw again the corpse-like face that had looked through the chink in the door.

"Wh—what do you mean?" he stammered. "I do not understand you."

His lips trembled. Was it possible, Dawtie wondered, that he had to do with the stealing of it?

The truth was this: he had learned of the existence of the cup from this very book, and he had never afterward rested until, after a search of more than ten years, he at length found it in the hands of a poor man who dared not offer it for sale. Once in his possession, the thought of giving it up, or of letting the owner redeem it, had never even occurred to him. Yet the treasure made him rejoice with a trembling that all his logic would have found it hard to explain. He would not confess to himself its real cause—namely, that his God-born essence was uneasy with a vague knowledge that it lay in the bosom of a thief.

"Don't you think, sir," said Dawtie, "that whoever has that

cup ought to send it back to the place it was stolen from?''

Had the old man been a developed hypocrite, he would have replied at once, ''He certainly should.'' But to condemn himself by word from his own mouth would have been to acknowledge that he ought to send the cup home, and that he dared not do. Men who will not do as they know make strange confusion in themselves. The worst rancor in the vessel of peace is the consciousness of wrong in a not all-unrighteous soul. The laird was false to his own self, but to confess himself false would be to initiate a change that would render life worthless to him. What would all his fine things be without their heart of preciousness, the one jewel that now was nowhere in the world but in his house, in the secret chamber of his treasures, which would be a rifled case without it? As is natural to one who will not do right, he began to argue the moral question, treating it as a point of analytical ethics that troubled the mind of the girl.

''I don't know that, Dawtie,'' he replied. ''It is not likely that the person who has the cup, whoever he may be—that is, if the cup still be in existence—is the same person who stole it. And it would hardly be justice to punish the innocent for the guilty—as would be the case if, supposing I had bought the cup, I had to lose the money I paid for it. Should the man who had not taken care of his cup have his fault condoned at my expense? Did he not deserve, one might say, to be so punished, placing huge temptation in the path of the needy, to the loss of their precious souls, and letting a priceless thing go loose in the world to work ruin to whoever might innocently buy it?''

His logic did not serve to reveal to him the falsehood of his reasoning, for his heart was in the lie.

''A score of righteous men may by this time have bought and sold the cup,'' he went on. ''And so, must the last meet the penalty, when the original owner, or some descendant of the man who lost it, chooses to claim it? For anything we know, he himself may have pocketed the price of the rumored theft. Can you not see it would be a flagrant injustice—fit indeed to put an end to all buying and selling? Possession would mean only strength to keep, and the world would fall into confusion."

"It would be hard, I grant," confessed Dawtie. "But the man who has it ought at least to give the head of the family in which it had been the chance of buying it back at the price it cost him. If he could not buy it back, then the thing would have to be thought over."

"I confess I don't see the thing," returned the laird. "But the question need not keep you out of bed, Dawtie. It is not often a girl in your position takes an interest in the abstract. Besides," he resumed, another argument occurring to him, "a thing of such historical value and interest ought to be where it was cared for, not where it was in danger every moment."

"There might be something in that," allowed Dawtie, "if it were where everybody could see it. But where is the good if it be but for the eyes of one man?"

The eyes she meant fixed themselves upon her till their gaze grew to a stony stare. She *must* know he had it! thought the laird. Or did she only suspect? He must not commit himself! He must set a watch on the door of his lips. What an uncomfortable girl to have in the house! Those self-righteous Ingrams! What mischief they did with their notions!

His impulse was to dart into his treasure cave, lock himself in, and hug the radiant chalice. But he dared not. He must endure instead the fastidious conscience and probing tongue of an intrusive maidservant!

"But," he rejoined, with an attempt at a smile, "if the pleasure the one man took in it should, as is easy to imagine, exceed immeasurably the aggregate pleasure of the thousands that would look upon it and pass it by—what then?"

"The man would enjoy it all the more that many saw it," answered Dawtie, "unless he loved it out of greed. If that were the case, he would be rejoicing in iniquity, for the cup would not be his. And anyhow, he could not take it with him when he died!"

The face of the miser grew grayer. His lip trembled, but he said nothing.

He was beginning to come close to hating Dawtie. She was an enemy! She sought nothing but his discomfiture, his misery. He had read strange things in certain old books, and half believed some of them. What if Dawtie were one of those evil powers that haunt a man in pleasant shape, learn the secrets of his heart, and gain influence over him that they may tempt him to yield his soul to the enemy?

She was set on ruining him! Certainly she knew that the cup was in his possession! He must *seem* to listen, but as soon as fit reason could be found that would neither compromise him nor offend her, she must be sent away. And she must never gain the means of proving what she now suspected!

He stood thinking. It was but for a moment, for the very next words from the lips of the girl who was to him little more than a house broom set him face to face with reality—the one terror.

"Eh, Master, sir," said Dawtie, with tears in her eyes and now at last breaking down in her English, "dinna ye *ken* that ye *hae* to give the man that aucht the gowden bicker the chance o' buyin' it back?"

The laird shivered. He dared not say "How do you know?" for he dared not hear the thing proved to him.

"If I had the cup," he began—but she interrupted him. It was time they should have done with lying!

"Ye ken ye hae the cup, sir!" she cried. "And I ken too, for I saw it in yer hands!"

"You shameless, prying hussy!" he shouted in a rage—but the tearful earnestness of her face made him think twice. It would not do to make an enemy of her. "Tell me, Dawtie," he said, with a sudden change of tone, "how was it you came to see it?"

She told him everything, and he knew that he had seen her see him in the middle of the night.

"All is not gold that glitters, Dawtie," he said. "The cup you saw was not the one in the book, but an imitation of it—mere gilded tin and colored glass—copied from the picture as near as they could make it—just to see what it must have been like. Why, my good girl, that cup would be worth thousands of pounds! So go to bed and don't trouble yourself anymore about gold cups. It is not likely any of them will come our way."

Simple and trusting as Dawtie was, she did not believe him. But she saw no good to be done by disputing what he ought to know.

"It wasna aboot the gold cup I was worried," she replied hesitatingly.

"You are right there!" he agreed, with another deathly laugh. "You have been worrying me about nothing half the night and I am shivering with cold. Both of us really must go to bed! What would your mistress say!"

"No, it wasna aboot the cup, gowd or no gowd," persisted Dawtie. "It was and is aboot my master I'm troubled! I'm terrible afraid for ye, sir. Ye're a worshiper o' mammon, and I can't help bein' feart for ye!"

The laird laughed, for the danger was over. To Dawtie's deep dismay, when confronted with what to her was an awful truth, he laughed!

"My poor girl," he said, "you take an innocent love of curious things for the worship of mammon! How could you believe an old man like me, an elder of the church, a dispenser of her sacred things, guilty of such an awful thing?"

He imagined her ignorantly associating the idea of some idolatrous ritual with what to him was but a phrase—the worship of mammon. "Do you not remember," he continued, "the words of Christ, that a man *cannot* serve God and mammon? If I be a Christian, as you will hardly doubt, it follows that I could not possibly be a worshiper of mammon, for the two cannot go together."

"But that's just it, sir," replied Dawtie, regaining her composure, and her English with it. "A man who worships God, worships him with his whole heart and soul and strength and mind. If he wakes at night, he thinks of God. If he is glad in his heart, it is because God is and because he knows that one day he shall behold his face. If a man worships God, he loves him so that no other love can come between him and God. If the earth were destroyed and the mountains cast into the middle of the sea, it would all be one to him, for God would be all the same. Is it not so, sir?"

"You are a good girl, Dawtie, and I agree with every word you say. It would be presumption to profess that I loved God to the point you speak of. But I deserve to love him. No doubt a man ought to love God so, and we are all sinners just because we do not love God so. But we have the atonement."

"But, sir," answered Dawtie, tears beginning to run down her cheeks once more, "I love God that way. Nothing matters without him. When I go to bed, I don't care if I never wake again in this world, for then I shall be where he would have me."

"I am afraid you are terribly presumptuous with God, Dawtie.—What if that should be in hell?"

"If it be, it will be the best. It will be to set me right. God is so good! When we're in his hands, what but good can possibly come of it? Tell me one thing, sir, when you die—"

"Tut, tut, lass! We're not come to that yet! There's no occasion to think about that for a while longer. We're in the hands of a reconciled God."

"What I want to know," pursued Dawtie, "is how you will feel when you haven't got anything."

"Not got anything, girl! Of course we shall want nothing then! I shall have to talk to the doctor about you. We shall have you killing us in our beds to know how we like it."

He laughed, but it was a rather scared laugh.

"What I mean," she persisted, "is—when you have no body and no hands to take hold of your cup, what will you do without it?"

"What if I leave it to you, Dawtie," returned the laird, with a stupid mixture of joke and avarice in his cold eye.

"Please, sir, I didn't say what would you do *with* it, but what would you do *without* it, when it will neither come out of your heart nor into your hands. It must be misery to a miser to *have* nothing!"

"A miser, hussy!"

"A lover of things more than a lover of God."

"Well, perhaps you have the better of me," he said after a cowed pause. He perceived there was no compromise possible with Dawtie. She knew perfectly what she meant, and he could neither escape her logic nor change her determination, whatever that might be. "I daresay you are right," he added. "I will think about what ought to be done about that cup."

He stopped. He had committed himself and as much as confessed the cup genuine!

But Dawtie had not been thinking just then about the cup at all, for she had not been deceived by anything the laird said. Giving up the cup would certainly not in itself kill the mammon-love in his heart. But it was plain that if he would consent to part with it for its money value, that would be a grand beginning toward the renouncing of dead things altogether. Such a step would begin turning toward the living one the love that now gathered, clinging and haunting, about gold cups and graved armor, and suchlike vapors and vanishings that pass with the sunsets and the snows.

"Oh, laird, laird!" she cried in purest entreaty. "Ye've been good and kind to me, and I love ye, the Lord kens! I pray ye for Christ's sake be reconciled to God, for ye hae been servin' mammon and not him, and ye hae jist said we canna serve the two; and what'll come o' it, only God can tell, but it *maun* be misery!"

Words failed her. She turned and left the room, with her apron held to her eyes.

The laird stood a moment like one lost, then went hurriedly into his so-called "closet" and shut the door. Whether he went on his knees to God as Dawtie did the moment she entered her room, or began again to gloat over his Cellini goblet, I do not know.

Dawtie cried herself to sleep, and came down in the morning

very pale. Her duty had left her exhausted, and with a kind of nausea toward all the ornaments and books in the house.

When breakfast time came and the laird appeared, he looked much the same as usual, only a little weary, which his daughter set down to his journey into town the day before. He revived, however, as soon as he had succeeded in satisfying himself that Alexa knew nothing of what had passed. How staid, discreet, and full of common sense Alexa seemed to him beside Dawtie, whose lack of education left her mind a waste swamp for the vagaries of whatever will-o'-the-wisp an overstrained religious fantasy might generate! But however much the laird might look the same as before, he could never, knowing that Dawtie knew what she knew, be again as he had been.

"You'll do a few of the books today, won't you, Dawtie," he said, "—when you have time? I never imagined I should be able to trust anyone with my books. I would sooner have old Meg shave me than let her dust an Elzevir! Ha, ha, ha!"

Dawtie was glad that at least he left the door open between them. She said that she would do a little dusting in the afternoon, and would be very careful. Then the laird rose and went out, and Dawtie noticed, with a shoot of compassion mingled with a mild remorse, that he had left his breakfast almost untouched.

But after that, far from ever beginning any sort of conversation with her, he seemed uncomfortable the moment they happened to be alone together. If he caught her eye, he would say—hurriedly, and as if acknowledging a secret between them—"By and by, Dawtie"; or, "I'm thinking about the business, Dawtie"; or, "I'm making up my mind, Dawtie," and so leave her. On one occasion he said, "Perhaps you will be surprised someday, Dawtie!"

Dawtie feared at times that she had done him harm rather than good by pressing upon him a duty that in the end he had not performed. But Andrew said, when she asked him about it, "If you believed you were supposed to speak to him, you must not trouble yourself about the result. That may be a thousand years off yet. You may have sent him into a hotter purgatory, and yet at the same time made it shorter for him. We know nothing but that God is righteous."

Dawtie was comforted, and things went on as before. Where people know their work and do it, life has few blank spaces for boredom and they are seldom to be pitied. Where people have not yet found their work, they may be more to be pitied than those that beg their bread. When a man knows his work and will not do it, pity him more than one who is to be hanged tomorrow.

16 / Questions

Andrew called on the laird to pay his father's rent, and Alexa, who had not seen him for some time, thought him improved in both carriage and speech.

She did not take into account his constant interaction with God, as with highest human minds, and his eager wakefulness to carry into action what things he learned. Thus trained in noblest fashions of freedom, it was small wonder that his bearing and matters, the natural outcome and expression of his habits of being, should grow in liberty. There was in them only the change of continued development.

Alongside such education as this, dealing with reality and inborn dignity, what mattered any amount of ignorance as to social custom! Society may judge its own; this man was not of it, and far surpassed what it would have regarded as its most accomplished pupils in all the essentials of breeding. The training may be slow, but it is perfect. To him who has yielded self, all things are possible. Andrew was aware of no difference. To himself he seemed the same as when a boy.

Alexa had not again alluded to his brother's letter concerning George Crawford, fearing he might say what she would find unpleasant. But now she wanted to get a definite opinion from him in regard to certain questions that had naturally of late occupied a good deal of her thought.

"What is your feeling concerning money lending, Mr. Ingram?" she said. "I mean at interest. I hear it is objected to by some religious teachers nowadays."

"It is by no means the first time in the world's history that objections to it have been raised," answered Andrew.

"But I want to know what *you* think of it, Mr. Ingram."

"I know little about any matter I have not had to deal with practically," replied Andrew.

"But shouldn't one have his ideas ready for the time when he will have to deal practically on one of them?" responded Alexa.

"I can see no use in making up my mind how to act in circumstances I am not in—and probably will never be in," answered Andrew. "I have enough to occupy me where I find myself. In thinking about circumstances foreign to me, duty is a comparatively feeble factor, being only duty imagined and not live duty, and the result is thus all the more questionable. The Lord instructed his apostles not to be anxious what they should say when they were brought before rulers and kings. So I too will leave the question of duty alone until action is demanded of me. In the meantime I will do the duty now required of me, which is the only preparation for the duty that is to come."

Although Alexa had not begun to understand Andrew, she had sense enough to feel that he was somehow ahead of her, and it was not likely he and George Crawford would be of one mind in the matter that occupied her. Their ways of looking at things were so different. Indeed, the very things the two men thought worth looking at were themselves so different.

She was silent for a moment, then said, "You can at least tell me what you think of gambling."

"I think it is the lowest mode of gaining or losing money a man could find."

"Why do you think so?"

"Because he desires only to gain, and can gain only by his neighbor's loss. One of the two must be the worse for his transaction with the other. Each *must* wish ill to his neighbor. Thus, to gamble at all, in any form, is of necessity to disobey the Lord's clear word that we are to do as we would be done by."

"But the risk was agreed upon between them."

"True—but in what hope? Was it not, on the part of each, that he would be the gainer and the other the loser? There is no common cause, nothing but pure opposition of interest."

"Are there not many things in which one must gain and the other lose?"

"There are many things in which one gains and the other loses. But if it is *essential* to any transaction that only one side shall gain, the thing is not of God. God's business transactions would see all sides gain, because all parties involved are seeking the good of the other, not themselves."

"What do you think of trading in stocks?"

"I do not know enough about it to have a right to speak."

"You can give your impression."

"I will not give what I do not value."

"Suppose, then, you heard of a man who had made his money in the stock market, how would you behave to him?

"I would not seek his acquaintance."

"If he sought yours?"

"Then the time might come to ask how he had made his money. Then it would be my business."

"What would make it your business?"

"That he sought my acquaintance. It would then be necessary to know something about him."

Alexa was silent for some time.

"Do you think God cares about everything?" she said at length.

"Everything," answered Andrew, and she said no more.

Andrew avoided the discussion of moral questions for mere discussion's sake. He regarded such discussion as *vermiculite,* and ready to corrupt the obedience. "When you have a thing to do," he would say, "you will do it right in proportion to your love of right. Do the truth and you will love the truth. For by doing it you will see it as it is, and no one can see the truth as it is without loving it. The more you *talk* about what is right, or even talk about doing it, the more danger you are in of turning it into unpracticed theory. Talk without action saps the very will. Something you have to do is waiting undone all the time you are talking, and getting more and more undone. The only refuge is *to do*.''

To know the thing he ought to do was a matter of import; to do the thing he ought to do was a matter of life and death to Andrew. He never allowed even a related question to force itself upon him until he had attended to the thing that demanded doing: it was merest common sense!

Alexa's correspondence with George had not been interrupted. But something, perhaps a movement from the world of spirit coming like the wind, had lately given her one of those motions toward betterment, which, however, occasioned, are the throb of the divine pulse in our life, the call of the Father, the pull of home, and the guide thither to such as will obey them. She had in consequence become somewhat doubtful about Crawford. This led to her talk with Andrew, which, while it made her think less of his intellect, influenced her in a way she neither understood nor even recognized.

There are two ways in which one nature may influence another for betterment: the one by strengthening the will, the other by heightening the ideal. Without even her suspicion of the fact, Andrew wrought in the latter way upon Alexa.

She grew more uneasy. Word was received that George was leaving New York and coming home. How was she to receive him? They were certainly not bound by engagement, yet they were on terms of intimacy. Was she to encourage the procession of that intimacy, or should she ward off any attempt at nearer approach?

17 / The Maker of Horses

George returned within the month and made an early appearance at Potlurg not many days later.

Dawtie met him in the court. She did not know him, but involuntarily shrank. There was a natural repugnance between them. The one was simple, the other double, the one pure, the other out for himself, the one loved her neighbor, the other preyed upon his.

George was a little louder and his manners more studied. Alexa felt him overblown. He was floridly at his ease. His dress was unobjectionable, and yet attracted notice; perhaps it was a little too considered. Alexa was disappointed, and a little relieved. He looked older, yet not more manly—and rather more plump about the waist and jowls. He had more of the confidence women dislike to see a man without than was pleasant, even to the confident Alexa. His speech was not a little infected with the nasality—as easy to catch as hard to get rid of—which I presume the Puritans carried from England to America. On the whole, George was less interesting than Alexa had expected.

He came toward her as if he would embrace her, but an instinctive movement on her part sufficed to check him. She threw an additional heartiness into her welcome, but kept him at arms' length. She felt as if she had lost an old friend, not gained a new one. He made himself very agreeable, but that he made himself thus made him less so.

There was more than these outward changes at work in Alexa's impression of George. There was still the underlying doubt concerning him. Although not yet a live soul, she had strong if vague ideas about right and wrong. And although she sought many things a good deal more than righteousness, she could not be considered an easy prey for what temptations might assail her. At the same time, she did not possess anything more than hundreds of thousands of well-meaning women to secure her from slow decay and final ruin.

They laughed and talked together very much like they used to, but both could feel there was a difference. George was stung by the sense of it—too much to show that he was annoyed. He laid himself out to be the more pleasing, as if determined to make her feel what he was worth—as the man, namely, whom he imagined himself and valued himself on being.

It is an argument for God to see what fools those make of themselves who, believing there is a God, do not believe *in* him—children who do not know the Father. Such make up the mass of churchgoers. Let an earthquake or a smallpox epidemic break loose around them and they will show what sort their faith is!

George had gotten rid of the folly of believing in the existence of a God, and naturally found himself more comfortable in consequence, for he never had believed in God, and it is awkward to believe and not believe at the same moment. What he had called his "beliefs" were as worthy of the name as those of most people, but whether he was better or worse without them hardly interests me, and my philanthropy will scarcely serve to make me glad that he was more comfortable.

As they talked, old times came up, and they drew a little nearer, until at last a gentle spring of rose-colored interest began a feeble flow in Alexa's mind. When George took his leave, which he did soon, with the wisdom of one who feared to bore, she went with him to the courtyard, where the gardener was holding the man's horse. Beside them stood Andrew, talking to the old man and admiring the beautiful animal in his charge.

"The life of the Creator has run free through every channel up to this creature!" he was saying as they came near.

"What rot!" said George to himself. But to Alexa he said, "Here's my old friend, the farmer, I declare!" Then to Andrew, "How are you, Mr. Ingram?"

He spoke as if they were old friends. "You seem to like the look of the beast," he went on. "*You* ought to know what's in horses!"

"He is one of the finest horses I ever saw," answered Andrew. "The man who owns him is fortunate."

"He ought to be a good one," said George. "I gave a hundred and fifty in guineas for him yesterday."

Andrew could not help vaguely reflecting upon what kind of money had bought him, if Sandy was right.

Alexa was pleased to see Andrew. He made her feel more comfortable. His presence seemed to protect her a little.

"May I ask you, Mr. Ingram," she said, "to repeat what you were saying about the horse as we came up?"

"I was saying," answered Andrew, "that, to anyone who understands a horse, it is clear that the power of God must have flowed unobstructed through many generations to fashion such a perfection."

"Oh, you endorse the evolutionary theory—do you?" remarked George. "I should hardly have expected that of a religious man like you!"

"I was only commenting on the horse itself. I do not think that has anything to do with what I said. No one disputes that this horse comes of many generations of horses. The evolution theory, if I understand it right, concerns itself with how his first ancestor in his own kind came to be a horse."

"And about that, what is your opinion?—that of Darwin, or that of the Bible?" said George.

"I do not see that they are in conflict," returned Andrew.

"How can you say that, with the scientists and the parsons arguing the case in their journals and pulpits from morning till night?"

"The only ones who argue are those who understand neither

the God of Genesis nor the science of the universe. The parsons make God too small to make use of science, the scientists make science so big they think it can function without God's having given it life. Both are wrong, for they do not grasp how big God truly is. The true debate is not over evolution, but over the simple question: How big is God? Is he big enough to use any means he chooses? And can life go without him?"

"So you understand what the world's learned men do not, Mr. Ingram?" said George, with more than a touch of sarcasm.

"I understand nothing of evolutionary theory," returned Andrew. "But I do know God. And I know he makes beautiful horses, whether he takes the one way or the other to make them, I am sure he takes the right way."

"You imply it is of little consequence what you believe about it."

"Very little indeed. You cannot imagine how little I care for the various opinions concerning abstract questions. If I had to make horses, my opinion would be of consequence. But as I do not, it matters nothing. But what I *do* think of consequence is this—that he makes them, not out of nothing, as the evolutionists would have it, if I understand them correctly, but out of *himself*. Why should my poor notion of God's *how* be of importance so long as when I see a horse like yours, Mr. Crawford, I say, God be praised! It is of eternal importance to love the animal and to love the man or woman who perhaps takes a different view on the question than I do, and to see them both in the beauty of the Lord. But it is of no importance whatsoever for me to fancy I know which way God took to make him. Not having in me the power or the stuff to make a horse, I cannot know how God made the horse. But I can know him to be beautiful!"

"You've not given up preaching and taken to the more practical side of life yet I see, Mr. Ingram!" said George.

Andrew laughed.

"I hope I have not ceased to be practical, Mr. Crawford. You are busy with what you see, and I am busy as well with what I don't see. Maybe you call my religion impractical, but all the time I believe my farm is in as good a state as your books."

George stole a look at the young farmer, but was satisfied he meant nothing by the remark. The self-seeker will step over the cliff into the very abyss of death, all the while protesting himself a practical man, and counting him unpractical who will not jump over the edge with him.

18 / The Shape of a Poem_____

With all his hard work on the farm, harder since Sandy left, Andrew continued to write, for he neither sought company nor drank strong drink nor was swept away by undisciplined passions. There were no demons riding the whirlwinds of his soul. It is not to be wondered at then that in time one of his poems should appear in print, nor that it was followed by others, which began, though nothing was known of their author, to attract notice and be talked about among certain influential, albeit small, literary circles.

It should therefore not come as a surprise to my reader to learn that about a year after George's return from New York, a small volume appeared, under the imprint of a well-reputed Edinburgh publishing house, bearing the name Andrew Ingram under its title. That the book was of genuine and original worth perhaps had little to do with the fact that it had the fortune to be favorably reviewed, given that scarcely one of those who reviewed the poem understood it, while all of them seemed to themselves to understand it perfectly. I mention the thing because had the book not been thus reviewed, Alexa would not have bought a copy or been able to admire it.

Though she did not see half what the passages quoted in the review involved, yet because Andrew had gotten a book published, and because she approved of certain lines, phrases, and passages in it—though chiefly because it had been praised by more than one influential paper—young Ingram rose immensely in Alexa's opinion. Despite the fact that he was the son of a tenant, was even a laborer on his farm, and had, without the gown of any university, covered a birth no higher than that of Jesus Christ, Alexa began, even against her own sense of what was fit, to look up to the ploughman.

The ploughman was not aware of it. And had he been he would have given it not a thought. He respected his landlord's daughter, and never once questioned her superiority as a lady where he made no claim to being a gentleman. But he recognized in her no power either to help or hurt.

When next they met, after her reading of the review and purchase of the volume of verse, Alexa was no longer indifferent to Andrew's presence, and even made a movement in the direction of being agreeable to him. Without even knowing she had ever used it, she in a measure dropped her patronizing carriage, and had the assurance to compliment him not merely on the poem he had written but on the way it had been received. Had Andrew told her how he felt, she would not have understood that he was as indifferent to the praise of what is called the public as if that public were indeed—what it is most like—a boy just learning to read. Yet it is the consent of such a public that makes the very essence of what is called fame! How should a man care for it who knows that he is on his way to join his peers, to be a child with the great ones of the earth, the lovers of the truth, the Doers of the Will! What to him will be the wind of the world he has left behind, a wind that cannot arouse the dead, that can only blow about the graveclothes of the dead as they bury their dead!

Andrew was neither annoyed nor gratified by the compliments Alexa paid him, for she was not yet able to feel what he cared for in his poetry—the thing that made him write it. But her gentleness and kindness did please him; he was glad to feel a little at home with her, glad to draw a little nearer to one who had never been other than good to him. And then, too, he appreciated her kindness, even her love, toward Dawtie.

"So, Andrew, you are a poet at last!" she said, holding out her hand to him, which Andrew received in a palm that wrote the better verse that it was gnarled with labor. "Please remember I was the first that found you out," she added.

"I think it was my mother," answered Andrew.

"And I would have helped you if you would have let me."

"Is it not wise though," said Andrew, "to push the bird off if he cannot sit safely on the edge of the nest?"

"Perhaps you are right. A failure then would have stood in the way of your coming fame."

"Oh, believe me, I do not care a short straw for that!"

"For what?"

"For fame."

"I think that is wrong of you, Andrew. We ought to care what our neighbors think of us."

"My neighbors did not set me to do the work, and I did not seek their praise in doing it. Their friendship I prize dearly, more than tongue can say, but not their praise."

"You surely cannot be so conceited, Andrew, as to think nobody capable of judging your work!"

"Far from it. But you were speaking of fame, and that does not come from any wise judgment."

"Then what do you write for if you care nothing for fame? I thought that was what all poets wrote for."

"So the world thinks, and sometimes those who do write for that reason have their reward."

"Tell me, then, what you do write for."

"I write because I want to tell something that makes me glad and strong. I want to say it, and so try to say it. Things come to me in gleams and flashes, sometimes in words themselves, and I want to weave them into a melodious, harmonious whole.

"I was once at an oratorio, and sitting there listening to it taught me the greatest lesson I have ever learned about the shape of a poem. In a pause of the music, I seemed all at once to see Handel's heavy countenance looking out of his great wig as he sat putting together his notes, ordering them about in his mind, and fixing in their places with his pen his drums and pipes and fiddles and roaring brass and flageolets and oboes and harps and french horns and cellos—all to open the door for the thing that was plaguing him with the confusion of its beauty. For I suppose even Handel did not hear it all clear and plain at first, but had to build his orchestra into a mental organ for his mind to let itself out by, through the many music holes, lest it should burst with its repressed harmonic delights. He must have felt an agonized need to set the haunting angels of sound in obedient order and range, responsive to the soul of the thing, its one ruling idea.

"I saw him with his white rapt face, looking like a prophet of the living God sent to speak out of the heart of the mystery of truth. I saw him as he sat staring at the paper before him, scratched all over as with the fury of a holy anger at his own impotence, and his soul communed with heavenliest harmonies.

"Now, will any man or woman persuade me that Handel at such a moment was athirst for fame? Or that the desire to please a roomful or even a worldful of such people as heard his oratorios gave him the power to write his music?

"No, Miss Fordyce. He was filled, not with the lust for fame, not with the longing for sympathy, and not even with the good desire to give delight, but with the music itself! It was crying in him to get out, and he heard it crying, and could not rest till he had let it out. And every note that dropped from his pen was a chip struck from the granite wall between the songbirds in their prison-nest and the air of their liberty. Creation is God's self-wrought freedom. No, ma'am, I do not despise my fellows, nor do I for a moment think myself above them or my work too good for their scrutiny. But neither do I prize the judgment of more than a few of them, even though I prize and love them for themselves. But I write for other reasons than their opinion."

Alexa was silent, and Andrew took his leave.

She sat still for a while thinking. If she did not grasp everything he said, at least she remembered Andrew's face as he talked. Surely neither presumption nor conceit could have made his face shine so!

19 / The Gambler and the Collector _____

For a time things got on very nicely with George.

He had weathered a crisis, had pulled himself back up, if not by the bootstraps then by the pocketbook, and was now full of confidence, as well as the show of it. That he thought himself a man who could do what he pleased was plain to everyone. His prosperity leaned upon that of certain princes of the power of money in America. Gleaning after them he found his fortune.

But he did not find much increase in favor with Alexa. Her spiritual tastes were growing more refined.

There was something about the man—nothing new, but of which she was gradually growing more aware—that she could no longer contemplate without dissatisfaction. It cost her tears at night to think that although her lover had degenerated, he had remained true to her. For she saw plainly that it was only lack of encouragement on her part that prevented him from asking her to be his wife. She must appear fickle and changeable, she thought. But was not, in fact, the change in him? This could hardly be the man she had been ready to love! True, the cause of his appearing different might lie in herself, but in any case he was not the gentleman she had thought him. Had she loved him, perhaps she would have stood by him bravely. But now she could not help recalling the disgrace of the father, and shrank from sharing it with the son.

It would hardly be any wonder, she thought, if the son proved less than honorable in the end as well.

Alexa would have broken it off altogether with George by

130

now but for one thing—he had come to be on very friendly terms with her father, and the laird enjoyed the man's company.

George had a large straggling acquaintance with things, and could readily appear to know more than he did. He had besides that, a most agreeable quality to a man with a hobby—he was a good listener, when he saw reason to be. He made himself so pleasant that the laird was not only always glad to see him but would often ask him to stay for supper, when he would fish up from the wine cellar he had inherited a bottle with a history and a character, and the two would pass the evening together. Alexa tried not to wish George away, for was not her poor old father happier for his company?

Though without much pleasure of his own in such things, moved by the reflection of the laird's interest, George even began to collect certain antiques a little, mainly in the hope of now and then picking up something that might gratify the laird; and he would not hesitate to spend a good sum when he came upon something he considered a good buy. Naturally the old man grew to regard him as a son of the best sort, one who would do anything to please his father and indulge his tastes.

George possessed a bulldog tenacity of purpose, as indeed his moneymaking indicated. And now he directed that same strength of will toward Potlurg and its laird, though Mr. Fordyce was hardly the primary target of his affections. For he saw himself in danger of losing Alexa, and concluded there were influences at work to the frustration of his own. He began to surmise that she doubted the character of his business dealings, and feared the clownish farmer-poet might have dazzled her womanly judgment with his new reputation. George naturally felt himself called upon to make good his position against any and every prejudice she might have conceived against him. He would yield nothing. If he was foiled in his pursuit of her, he was foiled; but it should not be his fault, and he would not throw in the sponge without a fight!

He had occasional twinges of discomfort over his recent past, for his conscience, although seared, was not seared as with the hottest iron, seeing he had never looked straight at any truth. In consequence, he vaguely imagined that it would ease those twinges if he could satisfy a good woman like Alexa sufficiently that she accepted not only him but also the money of which he had at such rare times a slight loathing. And then Alexa was good-looking—he thought her *very* good-looking!

George was so unlike Andrew, now that he began to imagine the farmer a competitor after Alexa's regard, how could he but dislike him? His dislike soon grew into jealousy, and then fostered into outright hatred. He called him a canting, sneaking fellow—which perhaps he was, if canting consists in giving God his own, and sneaking consists in fearing no man, in fearing nothing, indeed, but doing wrong. How could George consent even to the far-off existence of such a man!

The laird also—whether because of George or not, who can tell?—had taken a dislike to Andrew.

From the night when Dawtie made her appearance, Mr. Fordyce had not known an hour's peace. It was not that the episode had waked his conscience, though it had made it sleep a little less soundly. It was only that he feared she might take further action in regard to the cup. She seemed to him to be taking part with the owner of the cup against him. He could not see that she was taking part with him against the Devil. It could not have entered his self-absorbed mind that it was not the cup she was anxious about but the life of her master.

But the laird's anxiety was on an altogether different plane than Dawtie's.

What if she should tell the earl's lawyer all she knew, he thought. He would be dragged into public daylight! He could not pretend ignorance concerning the identity of the chalice; would not Dawtie bear witness that he had in his possession a book telling all about it!

But the girl of herself would never have turned against him. It was all that fellow Ingram, with his overstrained and absurd notions as to what God required of his poor sinful creatures!

Andrew did not believe in the atonement! He could not leave our
sins well enough alone and let Christ atone for them! He demanded more in the name of religion than any properly educated
minister ever would! And in his meddlesomeness had worried
Dawtie into doing as she did. She was a good and modest girl
and would never have acted this way on her own. Andrew was
over-righteous, eaten up with self-conceit and the notion of pleasing God more than other men! No doubt he held old grudges
against his former schoolmaster, and now was delighting in trying
to bring him to shame! Andrew was bent on returning evil for all
the good the laird had done him as a boy! He had not been a bad
boy at school. This change in him witnessed to the peril of ex-
tremes and religious fanaticism.

It was a happy thing young Crawford understood him! He
would be his friend and defeat the machinations of his enemy! If
only the fellow's lease were up, that he might evict him and get
rid of him for good!

Moved by George's sympathy with his tastes, the laird talked
more and more freely, and gradually drew nearer and nearer to
disclosing the possession that was the pride of his life. The enjoyment of a connoisseur or collector rests much on the glory of
possession—of having what another does not, or, better still, what
no other can possibly have. Yet to enjoy such possession alone is
to miss the triumph in such glory, which can only exist while
watching another's eyes widen at the display of what no other
man can call his own.

From what he had long ago seen on the night of the storm,
and now from the way the old man hinted and talked, and how
he occasionally broke off in mid-sentence as if catching himself
before revealing something, and also from the uneasiness the laird
sometimes manifested, George had guessed that there was something over whose possession he gloated, but for whose presence
among his treasures he could not comfortably account. He therefore set himself to try to make the laird unburden himself, if
possible without so much as asking a single question. A hold on

the father would be a hold on the daughter!

One day in a pawnbroker's shop, George lighted upon an old watch, a rarity indeed, which might or might not have the history attributed to it by the shopowner, but which was in itself more than interesting for the beauty of both material and workmanship. The sum asked for it was large, but with the chance of pleasing the laird, it seemed to George but a trifle. It was also, he judged, of intrinsic value from the mere worth of the stones and gold represented as a great part of the price. Had he been then aware of the passion of the old man for jewels in particular, he would have been all the more eager to secure it for him.

The watch was of good size, and by no means thin—a pocket alarm repeater, whose bell was dulled by the stones of the mine in which it lay buried. The gold case was one mass of gems of considerable size and every color. Ruby, sapphire, and emerald were judiciously parted by diamonds of utmost purity, while yellow diamonds took the golden place for which the topaz had not been counted of sufficient value. They were all crusted together as close as they could lie, the setting of them hardly showing. The face was of fine opals, across which moved the two larger hands radiant with rubies, while the second hand flitted flashing around, covered with tiny diamonds. The numerals were in sapphires, with a bordering ring of emeralds and black pearls. The jewel was a splendor of color and light.

The moment he had it in his possession, George called upon the laird.

Without preface, he took it from his pocket, held it a moment in the sunlight, and handed it to the laird.

Mr. Fordyce glowered at it with wide, hungry eyes. He saw an angel from heaven in a thing so compact, studded with tiny chips from the earth! As near as any *thing* can be loved by a live soul, the laird loved a fine stone. What in it he loved most—the color, the light, the shape, the value, the mystery—he could not have told. And here was a jewel of many fine stones!

With both hands he pressed it to his bosom. Then he held it

up to the light and looked at it in the sun. Then he walked into the shadow of the house, for they had met outside in the garden, and looked at it again.

Suddenly he thrust it into his pocket, and hurried, followed by George, into the house and directly to his study. There he closed the shutters, lit a lamp, pulled out the marvel, and gazed at it again, turning it in all directions. At length he laid it on the table and sank with a sigh into a chair. George understood the sigh, and dug its source deeper by telling him, as he had heard it, the story of the watch.

"It may be true," he said as he ended. "I remember some time ago seeing a description of it in a book or magazine. I think I could lay my hand on it."

"Would you mind leaving it with me till you come again?" faltered the laird.

He knew he could not buy it—he hadn't the money. But he would gladly dally with the notion of being its possessor. To part with it, the moment after having held it in his hand and gloated over it for the first time, would be too keen a pain. It was unreasonable to have to part with it at all, he thought. He *ought* to be its owner! Who could be such an owner to a thing like that as he! It was wrong that it was not his. Next to his cup, it was the most precious thing he had ever wished to possess!—a thing for a man to take to the grave with him!

Was there *no* way of carrying *any* treasure to the other world? He would have sold a piece of his land if he thought he could secure the little pocket miracle, but, alas, it was all entailed and he was not at liberty to do so! For a moment even the Cellini chalice seemed of less account, and he felt ready to throw open the window of his treasure-room and pitch everything out. The demon of *having* is as imperious and as capricious as that of drink, and there is no refuge from it but with the Father. "This kind goeth not out but by prayer."

The poor slave uttered, not now a sigh, but a groan, "You'll tell the man," he said, thinking George had borrowed the thing to show him, "that I did not even ask the price. I know I cannot buy it!"

"Perhaps he would give you credit," suggested George with a smile.

"No, I will have nothing to do with credit! I would not be able to call it my own!"—Money-honesty was strong in the laird.—"But," he continued, "do try and persuade him to let me have it for a day or two—that I may get its beauty by heart, and think of it all the days and dream of it all the nights of my life after this."

"There will be no difficulty about that," answered George. "I know the owner well, and he will be delighted to let you keep it as long as you wish."

"If only it were so."

"It *is* so."

"You—you don't mean—?"

"That is precisely what I mean," laughed George good-naturedly. "I am the owner of the watch!"

"You—you—" stammered the laird; "—this queen of jewels is yours, George, and you will lend it to me!"

"The thing is mine, but I will not lend it—not even to you, sir."

"I don't wonder!—no, not for a moment! It is far too valuable! But it is a great disappointment. I was beginning to hope I—I—might have the loan of it for a week, or even two."

"I would be happy to let you if the thing were mine," said George, toying with him, "but—"

"Oh, I beg your pardon. I thought you said it was yours."

"So it was when I brought it here, but it is mine no longer. It is yours. I purchased it for you this morning."

The old man was speechless.

He rose, seized George by both hands, and stood staring at him. Something very much like tears gathered within the reddened rims of his eyes. He had grown paler and feebler lately, ever in vain devising secure possession of the cup—possession moral as well as legal. But this entrancing gift brought with it strength and hope in regard to the chalice. "To him that hath shall be given," quoted the god mammon within him.

"George!" he said with a moan of ecstasy, "you are my good angel!" and he sat down exhausted.

The watch indeed, as he had hoped, proved to be George's key to the laird's "closet," as he persisted in calling his treasury.

In old times not a few houses in Scotland held a certain tiny room, built for the head of the family, to be his closet for prayer. It was, I believe, with the notion of such a room in his head that the laird had called his museum his closet. And he was more right than he meant to be, for in that chamber he did his truest worship—truest as to the love in it, falsest as to its object. For there he worshiped the god vilest bred of all the gods, bred namely of man's distrust in the Life of the universe.

And now two began to meet together for worship. For from this time forward the laird, at length disclosing his secret, gave George access to his sanctuary.

By this time George was able to take a genuine interest in the collection. But he was much amused, sometimes annoyed, with the behavior of the old man in his closet. He was more nervous and touchy over his things than a she-bear over her cubs.

Of all the dangers to his darlings, he thought a woman the worst. Therefore, almost the moment he had first entered it, he had spied the possibility of making the room a hidden one, and had avidly seized it at once. The work had been carried out before Alexa had ever known the house once had a dining room. And until Dawtie had disturbed him in the middle of the night, no woman's eyes had since laid eyes on the place.

The laird now became, if possible, fonder of his things than ever, and flattered himself that he had found in George a fellow worshiper. George's pretended appreciation enhanced his sense of their value.

20 / A Conversation on the Moor _____

Alexa had a strong shaggy pony, which she now rode the oftener that George came to visit so frequently. She always took care to be gone well before he arrived on his beautiful horse.

One lovely summer evening she had been across the moor a long way, and was returning as the sun went down. A glory of red molten gold shone in her face and she could see nothing in front of her. She was therefore a little startled when a voice greeted her from out of the light with a respectful good evening. A moment later and she was alongside the speaker in the blinding veil of the sun. It was Andrew walking home from a village on the other side of the moor. She drew rein, and they went along together.

"What has come over you, Mr. Ingram?" she said. "I hear you were at church last Sunday evening!"

"Why should I not be?" asked Andrew.

"For the same reason that you are not in the habit of going."

"There might be a good reason for going once, or for going many times, and yet not for going always."

"We won't begin with quarreling! There will always be things we shall not agree about."

"Yes, one or two—for a time, I believe," returned Andrew.

"So, what did you think of Mr. Rackstraw's sermons? I suppose you went to hear *him,* knowing of his wide reputation?"

"Yes, ma'am—at least partly."

"Well?"

"Before I answer, will you tell me first whether you were

138

satisfied with Mr. Rackstraw's teaching?"

"I was quite satisfied."

"Then I see no reason for saying anything about it."

"If I am wrong, you ought to try to set me right."

"The prophet Elisha would have done no good by throwing his salt into the running stream. You will remember, he cast it into the spring."

"I do not understand you."

"There is no use in persuading a person to change an opinion."

"Why not?"

"Because the man is neither the better nor the worse for it. If you had told me you were distressed to hear a man in authority speak as Mr. Rackstraw spoke concerning a being you loved, I would have tried to comfort you by pointing out how false his view of our Father is. But if you are content to hear God so represented, why should I seek to convince you of what is valueless to you? Why offer you to drink what your heart is not thirsting after? Would you love God more because you found he was not what you were quite satisfied he should be?"

"Please tell me more plainly what you mean?"

"You must excuse me. I have said all I will. I cannot reason in defense of God. It seems blasphemy to argue that his nature is not such as no honorable man could love in another man."

"But if the Bible says so?"

"If the Bible said so, the Bible would be false. But the Bible does not say so."

"How is it, then, that it seems to say so?"

"Because you were taught falsely about him before you desired to know him."

"Taught by whom?"

"By the generations of so-called teachers and writers and clergymen and self-appointed interpreters of truth, who place their own limited and restrictive viewpoints about a being they call their god above the loving character, indeed the very essence, of our *true* God, the Father of Jesus Christ."

"But I am capable of judging such things now for myself."

Andrew was silent.

"Am I not?" insisted Alexa.

"Do you desire to know God?" asked Andrew.

"I think I do know him."

"And you think those things true?"

"Yes."

"Then we are where we were a moment ago, and I say no more."

"You are not polite, Andrew!"

"I cannot help it. I must let you alone to believe about God what you can. You will not be blamed for not believing what you cannot."

"Do you mean that God never punishes anyone for what he cannot help?"

"Assuredly. God will punish only for wrong choices we make. And then his punishment will be redemptive, not retributive, to make us capable—more than merely capable; hungry, aching, yearning to be able—to make *right* choices, so that in the end we make that one supreme right choice our wills were created to make—the joyful giving up of our wills into *his*!"

"How do you prove that?"

"I will not attempt to prove it. If you are content to think of God as a being of retribution, if it does not trouble you that your God should be so unjust, then it would be fruitless for me to try to prove otherwise to you. We could discuss the question for years and only make enemies of ourselves. As long as you are satisfied with such a god, I will not try to dissuade you. Go on thinking so until at last you are made miserable by it. Then I will pour out my heart to deliver you from the falsehoods taught you by the traditions of the elders."

"Is that not a term Jesus applied to the teaching of the Pharisees?"

"We in this modern age have hundreds of our own traditions

of the elders that keep us from seeing God's face as surely as those ancient regulations did the Pharisees.''

Alexa was struck, not with any truth in all he said, but with the evident truthfulness of the man himself. Right or wrong, there was that about him—a certain radiance of conviction—which certainly was not about Mr. Rackstraw.

"The things that can be shaken," said Andrew, as if thinking with himself, "may last for a time. But they will at length be shaken to pieces, so that the things which *cannot* be shaken may emerge as what they truly are. Whatever we call religion will vanish when we see God face to face.''

For a while they went brushing through the heather in silence.

"May I ask you one question, Mr. Ingram?'' said Alexa at length.

"Surely. Ask me anything.''

"And you will answer me?''

"If I am at liberty to answer you, I will.''

"What do you mean by being at liberty? Are you under some vow?''

"I am under the law of love. I am bound to do nothing to hurt. An answer that would do you no good, I will not give.''

"How do you know what will or will not do me good?''

"I must use what judgment I have.''

"Is it true, then, that you believe God gives you whatever you ask?''

"I believe God answers all prayer," replied Andrew, "but the shape of the answer depends largely upon the heart of the person praying. Selfish prayers he must doubtless answer differently than selfless prayers. For myself, I have never asked anything of him that he did not give me.''

"Would you mind telling me anything you have asked of him? Do you pray for rain for your crops or for your book to sell in great quantities?''

Andrew laughed. "Such things I do not pray for. God is not a genie in a bottle to satisfy our earthly desires.''

"What do you pray for, then?"

"I have never yet required to ask anything not included in the prayer, 'Thy will be done!' "

"That will be done without your praying for it."

"Perhaps if you view those words of Christ's as a vague general prayer that somehow or other God's will in the universe will be done, I suppose you are right. But that prayer is far more personal than most people realize. And thus I do *not* believe it will be done, to all eternity, in the place where it needs doing the most, without my praying for it."

"Where is that?"

Andrew was silent a moment, thinking. Then he continued.

"Where first I am accountable that his will should be done?" he asked. "Is it not in myself . . . in my own heart? And how is his will to be done in *me* without *my* willing it? Does he not want me to love what he loves?—to be like himself?—to do his will with the glad effort of my will?—in a word, to will what he wills? And when I find I cannot, what am I to do but pray for help? I pray, and he helps me."

"There is nothing so strange in that!"

"Surely not. It seems to me the simplest of common sense. It is my business, the business of every man, every woman, every child, that God's will be done by their obedience to that will the moment they know it."

"I fancy you are not so different from other people as you think yourself. But they say you want to die."

"I want only what God wants."

"So you don't care if you live or die?"

"I love life—whether I live it here or there matters little. I desire righteousness."

"Then you accept the righteousness of Christ?"

"Accept it! I long for it."

"You know that is not what I mean! Do you accept the blood of Christ as your only righteousness?"

"I seek first the kingdom of God and God's righteousness."

"You are avoiding my question! Do you accept the righteousness of Christ and the shedding of his blood on the cross instead of your own?"

"I have no righteousness of my own to put it instead of. The only righteousness there is, is God's, and he will make me righteous like himself. That is his plan in the universe, throughout all eternity. He is not content that his one son only should be righteous. He wants all his children to be righteous as he is righteous. He is making sons and daughters after his own kind. The thing is plain. I will not argue about it."

"You do not believe in the atonement!"

"I believe in Jesus Christ. He *is* the atonement. What strength God has given me I will spend in knowing him and trying to do what he tells me, not in trying to analyze and understand and argue about his means and ways and *how* Jesus atones for us. To attempt to interpret his plans before we know him is to mistake both him and his plans. I know this, that he has given his life for what multitudes who call themselves by his name would not rise from their pews to share in!"

"You think me incapable of understanding the gospel."

"I think if you did understand the Gospel—the Good News— of Christ, you would be incapable of believing the things about his Father that you say you do believe. What 'good' is there in Mr. Rackstraw's gospel of a vengeful god-king on his throne of retaliatory judgment? That seems to me anything but good news! But I will not say a word more. When you are able to see the truth, you will see it, and when you desire the truth, you will be able to see it."

Alexa touched her pony with her whip. But by and by she pulled him up and made him walk till Andrew overtook her.

The sun was by this time far out of sight, the glow of the west was over, and twilight lay upon the world. Its ethereal dimness had sunk into her soul.

"Does the gloaming make you sad, Mr. Ingram?" she asked.

"It makes me very quiet," he answered, "—as if all my people were asleep and waiting for me."

"Do you mean as if they were all dead? How can you talk of it so quietly?"

"Because I do not believe in death."

"What *do* you mean?"

"I am a Christian."

"I should hope so, Mr. Ingram! Though to be honest with you, some things you say make me doubt it. Perhaps you would say I am not a Christian!"

"It is enough that God knows whether you are a Christian or not. Why should I say you are or are not?"

"But I want to know what you meant when you said you were a Christian. How should that make you indifferent to the death of your friends? Death is a dreadful thing however you look at it."

"The Lord says, 'He that liveth and believeth in me, shall never die.' If my friends are not dead, but living and waiting for me, why should I think of joining them only on a fierce, stormy night, or during a black frost, instead of in the calm of such a sleeping day as this—a day with the sun hid, as Shakespeare calls it."

"How you do mix things up! Shakespeare and Jesus Christ!"

"God mixed them up first, and will mix them a good deal more yet," said Andrew.

Except for the smile that would hover like a heavenly angel about his mouth, his way of answering would sometimes have seemed curt to those who did not understand him. Instead of holding aloof in his superiority, however, as some thought he did when he would not answer, or answered abruptly, Andrew's soul would be hovering, watching and hoping for a chance of lighting, and giving of the best he had. He was like a great bird changing parts with a child—the child afraid of the bird, and the bird enticing the child to be friends. He had learned that if he poured out his treasure recklessly, it might be received with dishonor, and but choke the way of the chariot of approaching Truth.

"Perhaps you will say next there is no such thing as suffering," resumed Alexa.

"No, the Lord said that in the world his friends should have tribulation."

"What tribulation could you possibly have in your life—you, who are so specially his friend?"

"Not much yet. It is a little, however, to know these things I have been speaking to you about—such strong, beautiful, and happy-making things—and all the time my people, my beloved humans, born of my Father in heaven, with the same heart for joy and sorrow, will not listen and be comforted and come face-to-face with their very Father. I think that was what made our Lord sorriest of all."

"I have no patience with you, Mr. Ingram! How can you possibly dare liken your troubles to those of our Lord—making yourself equal with him!"

"Is it making myself equal with him to say that I understand a little how he felt toward his fellowmen? I am always trying to understand him. Would it be a wonder if I did glean a little sometimes? How is a man to do as *he* did without gradually coming to know him?"

"Are you going to work miracles next?"

"Jesus was always doing what God wanted him to do. That was what he came for, not to work miracles. He could have worked a great many more if he had pleased, but he did no more than God wanted of him. Am I not to try to do the will of God, because he who died that I might, always succeeded however hard it was, and I am always failing and having to try again? Should I not constantly be trying to obey God more perfectly? Should I not be attempting to model my life after that of Jesus? Is not the sum of life to do what God wants us to, exactly as Jesus did?"

"And you think you will come to such perfection in this life?"

"I never think about that. I only think about doing his will now—not about doing it then—that is, tomorrow, or the next day, or in the next world. I know only one life—the life that is hid with Christ in God—and that is the life by which I live here and now."

"Now you sound like a theologian."

"No theology or doctrines for me! I do not make schemes of life—I only want to *live*. Life will teach me God's plans. I will take no trouble about them. I will only obey, and then receive the bliss he sends me. And of all things, I will not make theories of God's plans and methods for other people to accept. I will only do my best to destroy such theories as I find coming between some poor gloomy heart and the sun shining in his strength. Those who love the shade of lies, let them walk in it until the shiver of the eternal cold drives them to seek the face of Jesus Christ. To appeal to their intellect would be but to drive them all the deeper into the shade to justify their being in it. And if by argument you did happen to persuade them out of it, they would but run into a deeper and worse darkness."

"How could that be?"

"They would at once think that by an intellectual stride, they had advanced in the spiritual life, whereas in reality they would be neither the better nor the worse. I know a man, once among the foremost in denouncing the tenets of the old theology, who is now no better than a swindler."

"You mean—"

"No one you know, Miss Fordyce. His intellectual freedom seems only to have served his spiritual subjugation. Right opinion except it spring from obedience to the truth is but so much rubbish on the golden floor of the temple. Being doctrinally correct, even down to every detail, avails *nothing* in a man's heart and will— and it is only there that unity with our Maker begins."

The peace of the night and its luminous earnestness were gleaming on Andrew's face. Glancing up as he ceased, Alexa felt again the inroad of a sense of something in the man that was not in the other men she knew—the spiritual shadow of a dweller in regions beyond her knowledge. The man was ahead of her, indeed out of her sight!

The whole thing was too simple for her. Only a child could understand it. Instead of listening to the elders and priests to learn how to save his soul, he cast away all care of himself, left that to God, and gave himself to do the will of him from whose heart he came, even as the eternal Life, the Son of God, required of him. In him throbbed the mighty hope of becoming one mind, heart, soul, one eternal being, with him, with the Father, with every good man, with the universe that was his inheritance. He walked in the world as Enoch walked with God, held by his hand. This is what man was and is meant to be, what man must become. Thither the wheels of time are roaring. Thither work all the silent potencies of the eternal world, and they that will not awake and arise from the dead must be flung from their graves by the throes of a shivering world.

When he was done speaking, Andrew stood and looked up. A few stars were looking down through the limpid air.

Alexa rode on. Andrew let her go, and walked after her alone, sure that her mind must one day open to the eternal fact that God is all in all, the perfect friend of his children.

21 / When Hearts Are as Open as Faces___

Alexa kept hoping that George would realize she was not inclined toward him as she had been, and that, instead of bringing the matter up openly between them, he would continue to come and go merely as the friend of her father.

But George would not simply let it drop. He came to the conclusion that he ought to remain in doubt about her feelings no longer. Therefore, one afternoon when he happened to be there, he followed her into the garden.

She had gone there with a certain half scientific, half religious book in her hand, from which she was storing her mind with arguments against what she supposed the opinions of Andrew. She had, however, little hope of his condescending to front them with counter-argument. His voice constantly returned to the ear of her mind in words like this: *If you are content to think so, you are in no condition to receive what I have to communicate. Why should I press water on a soul that is not thirsty? Let us wait for the draught of the desert, when life is a low fever and the heart is dry, when the earth is like iron and the heavens above it are as brass!*

Absorbed in thought, she gave a little jump out of her seat at the sound of George's voice.

"What lovely weather!" he said.

Even lovers betake themselves to the weather as a medium—the side of nature that all understand. It was a good, old-fashioned, hot, heavy summer afternoon, one ill-chosen for lovemaking.

"Yes?" answered Alexa, with a point of interrogation subaudible, and held her book so that he might feel it on the point of being lifted again to eager eyes. But he was not more sensitive than sentimental.

"Please put your book down for a moment," he said. "I have not lately asked too much of your attention, Alexa."

"You have been very kind, George," she answered.

"Kind in not asking much of your attention?"

"Yes—that, and giving my father so much of yours."

"I certainly have seen more of him than of you!" returned George, hoping her words meant reproach. "But he has always been kind to me and seems pleased to see me. And you have not given me much encouragement since my return from the States."

To begin a would-be confession of love with a complaint is not wise, and George knew immediately that he had gotten off into the wrong track. But Alexa took care that he should not get out of it easily. Not being simple, he always tried to think and scheme about what was the best course to pursue, and often went wrong. The man who cares only for what is true and right is saved much thinking and planning. He generally sees but one way of doing a thing.

"I am glad to hear you say so, George. You have not mistaken me."

"You were not so sharp with me when I went away, Alexa!"

"No. Then you were going away."

"Should you not show a fellow some kindness when he comes back?"

"Not when he does not seem content with having come back!"

"I do not understand."

But Alexa gave no explanation.

"Are you saying you would be kind to me if I were going away again?"

"Perhaps."

"That is, if you were sure I was not coming back."

"I did not *say* that."

"I can't make you out, Alexa! I used to think there could never be any misunderstanding between you and me. But something has crept in between us, and for the life of me I don't know what it is! Someone has no doubt been maligning me to you!"

"The testimony against you is from your own lips, George. I heard you talking to my father and was aware of a tone I did not like. I listened more attentively and became convinced that your ways of thinking had deteriorated. There seemed not a remnant left of the honor I used to think one of your chief characteristics."

"Why, certainly, as an honest man, I cannot talk religion like your friend the farmer! Do you hold that against me?"

"Do you mean that Andrew Ingram is not an honest man?" rejoined Alexa with some heat.

"I mean that I am an honest man."

"Why then am I doubtful of you?"

"I can tell the quarter from which that doubt was blown!"

"It would be of greater consequence to blow it away!—But tell me, George Crawford, do you sincerely believe yourself an honest man?"

"As men go, yes."

"But not as men go, George. That is not what I mean. That is as good as to say that you would count it honesty if all men were equally dishonest together. What I mean is this: Do you believe yourself an honest man as you would like to appear to the world when hearts are as open as faces?"

He was silent.

"Would the way you have made your money stand the scrutiny of—? She had Andrew in her mind and was on the point of saying "Jesus Christ," but she felt she had no right. She hesitated briefly.

"—of our friend Andrew?" supplemented George, with a spiteful laugh. "The only honest mode of making money he knows is the strain of his muscles—the farmer way! He wouldn't even hold on to his grain an extra month for a better market—not he!"

"It so happens that you are exactly correct about that, for he and my father had a dispute on that very point, and I heard them. He said poor people were not to go hungry that he might get rich.

He was not sent into the world to make money, he said, but to grow corn and wheat and barley and oats. The grain was grown, and he could get enough for it now to live by, and he had no right and no desire to get more—and would not store it to play the market. The land was God's, not his, and the poor were God's children, and they had their rights from him; they were God's hungry, the land was God's provision, and he was God's provider. He was sent to grow grain for them."

"And what did your father say to that wisdom?"

"That is no matter. Nor do I profess to understand Mr. Ingram. I only know," added Alexa with a little laugh, "that he is consistent, for he has puzzled me all my life. However, I can see a certain nobility in him that sets him apart from other men."

"And I can see that when I left I was needlessly modest! I thought *my* position in the world too humble!"

"What am I to understand by that?"

"Exactly what you think I mean."

"I wish you a good afternoon, Mr. Crawford!"

Alexa rose and left him.

George had indeed grown coarser! He turned where he stood with his hands in his pockets and watched her go, then smiled to himself—a somewhat nasty, self-important smile—and said, "At least I made her angry, and that's something! She's not totally indifferent to me yet! Poet indeed! What has a fellow like that to give her? He's not even the rustic gentleman type! A clodhopper born and bred! But his father's lease will soon be up, so I've heard, and the laird will never renew it to *him*! He hates the canting scoundrel!"

On Alexa's part, George's behavior now put Andrew's manners in an altogether more favorable light. Though he never said a word to flatter Alexa, often spoke in a way she did not like at all, and persistently refused to enter into argument with her, all the while his every tone, every movement toward her was full of respect. And however she strove against the idea, she could not help feeling him her superior, and indeed began to wish that she had never shown herself at a disadvantage by the assumption of superiority. She began to feel that as she disapproved of George, and could not like him, so the young farmer disapproved of her.

It was a new and by no means agreeable thought. Andrew delighted in beautiful things, but he did not see anything beautiful in her! Alexa was not conceited, but she knew she was handsome. She knew also that Andrew would never feel one heartthrob more because of any such beauty as hers.

It would be something to be loved by a man like that! But Alexa was too maidenly to think of trying to make any man love her—and even if he did grow to love her, she could never marry a man in Andrew's position! She might stretch a point or two were the difference between them but a point or two. But there was no stretching points to the marrying of a peasant, without education, who worked on his father's farm! The thing was ridiculous!—of course she knew that!—the very idea too absurd to pass through her idlest thoughts!

But she was not going to marry George! That much was settled! In a year or two he would be quite fat. And he always had his hands in his pockets. There was something about him not like a gentleman. He had the appearance instead of an auctioneer!

She took her pony and went for a ride.

But George had no intention of forsaking the house—not yet, at least. He was bent on humbling his cousin. Therefore, he continued his relations with her father, while he hurried on, as fast as could be done with good masonry, with the building of a house on a small estate he had bought in the neighborhood, intending it to be such as must be an enticement to any lady. So long had he looked at everything through the veil of money that he could not think even of Alexa without thinking of mammon as well. By this time also he was so much infected with the old man's passion for curious and valuable things that the idea of one day calling the laird's wonderful collection his own had a real part in his desire to become the laird's daughter's husband.

He *would not* accept her dismissal as final!

22 / The Heart of the Heart

The laird had been doing poorly for several weeks, and Alexa began to fear that he was failing.

Nothing more had passed between him and Dawtie, but it was clear the incident with her continued to haunt him and was the source of his weakening condition. He knew that Dawtie's anxious eyes were often watching him, and the thought worried him not a little.

As for Dawtie, her thoughts and prayers constantly hovered about the person of the laird, whom she grew to love more and more with true daughterly affection. If he would but make a start, she thought, and not lose all the good of this life. It was too late for him to rise very high, she knew. He would never on earth be a saint, but he might at least set a foot on the eternal stair that leads to the fullness of bliss. He would have a sore fight with all those imps of things before he ceased to love that which was not lovely and to covet that which was not good. But the man who could repent before he left this world gained one of the most precious benefits it has to offer! If only the laird would start up the hill before his body got all the way to the bottom!

Was there any way to approach him again with her petition, Dawtie wondered, to encourage him to be good to himself, good to God, good to the universe, to love what was worth loving and cast away what was not? She had no light on what to do and could therefore do nothing.

Suddenly the old man failed altogether—apparently from no cause but weakness. The unease of his mind, the haunting of the dread thought of having to part with the chalice, had induced it.

He was in his closet one night late into the morning, and the next day did not get up for breakfast. He wanted a little rest, he said. In a day or two he would be fine! But the hour to rise the next morning came, and still he lay in bed. He seemed very troubled at times, and very desirous of getting up, but was never able to.

It soon became necessary to sit with him at night. In fits of delirium he would make fierce attempts to rise, insisting that he must go to his study. He never mentioned his closet. Even in dreams his secrecy was dominant. Dawtie, who had her share in nursing him, kept hoping her opportunity would come. He did not seem to hold any resentment against her. His illness would protect him, he thought, from further intrusion of her conscience upon his. She must know better than to irritate a sick man with her meddling! Everybody could not be a saint! It was enough to be a Christian like other good and salvable Christians. It was enough for him if through the merits of his Savior he gained admission to the heavenly kingdom at last!

He never thought how, once in, he could bear to stay in. It never occurred to him that heaven would be to him the dullest place in the universe of God, more wearisome than the kingdom of darkness itself. And all the time the young woman with the savior-heart was watching by his bedside, ready to speak. But the Spirit gave her no utterance, and her silence soothed his fear of her.

One night he was more restless than usual. Waking from his troubled slumber, he called her—in the tone of one who had something important to communicate.

"Dawtie," he said with a feeble voice but glittering eye, "there is no one I can trust like you. I have been thinking of what you said ever since that night. Go to my closet and bring me the cup."

Dawtie debated with herself momentarily whether to obey him would be right. But she reflected that it made little difference whether the object of his passion was in his hand or in his chest of valuables while it was all the same deep in his heart. And his words implied that he might want to take his farewell of it. So she said, "Yes, sir," and stood waiting.

He did not speak.

"I do not know where to find it," she added.

"I will tell you," he replied, but seemed to hesitate.

"I will not touch a single thing besides," said Dawtie.

He believed her, and at once proceeded.

"Take my bunch of keys from the hook behind me."

She did so. He took them and fumbled with them a moment.

"There is the key to the closet door. And there, the commonest looking key of the whole bunch, but in reality the most cunningly devised, is the key to the cabinet I keep it in!"

Then he told her where, behind a little bookcase that moved from the wall on hinges, she would find the cabinet, and in what part of it the cup would be, wrapped up in a piece of silk that had once been a sleeve worn by Madame de Genlis—which fact did not make Dawtie much wiser.

She went, found the chalice, and brought it to where the laird lay straining his ears and waiting for it as a man at the point of death might await the sacramental cup from the absolving priest.

His hands trembled as he took it, for they were the hands of a lover—strange as that love was, which not merely looked for no return but desired to give neither pleasure nor good to the thing loved. It was not a love of the merely dead, but a love of the unliving!

He pressed the thing to his bosom. Then, as if rebuked by the presence of Dawtie, he put it a little away from him and began to pore over every stone, every repoussé figure between, and every engraved ornament around the gems, each of which he knew the shape, order, and quality of color better than ever he knew the face of wife or child. But soon his hands sank on the counterpane of silk patchwork, and he lay still, grasping tightly the precious thing.

All at once he woke with a start and a cry, but found it safe in both his hands.

"You didn't try to take the cup from me—did you, Dawtie!"

"No, sir," answered Dawtie. "I would never take it out of your hand, but I *would* be glad to take it out of your heart."

"If only they would bury it with me!" he murmured, heedless of her words.

"Oh, sir! Do you want it burning your heart to all eternity? Give it up, laird, and take instead the treasure that no thief can ever steal."

"Yes, Dawtie, yes! That is the true treasure!"

"And to get it we must sell all we have."

"He gives and withholds as he sees fit."

"No, laird. To get that treasure we must give up this world's."

"I'll not believe it!"

"And then, when you go down into the blackness, longing for the cup that you will never see again, you will complain that God would not give you the strength to fling it from you?"

He hugged the chalice as he replied. "Fling it from me!" he cried fiercely. "Girl, who are you to torment me before my time!"

"God gives every man and woman the power to do what he requires, and we are fearfully to blame for not using the strength God gives us."

"I cannot bear the strain of thinking!" gasped the laird.

"Then give up thinking, and do the thing! Or shall I take it for you?"

She put out her hand as she spoke.

"No! no!" he cried, grasping the cup tighter. "You shall not touch it! You would give it to the earl! I know you! Saints hate what is beautiful!"

"I like better to look at things in my Father's hand than in my own."

"You want to see my cup—it *is* my cup!—in the hands of that spendthrift fool, Lord Borland!"

"It is in the Father's hand, whoever has it."

"Hold your tongue, Dawtie, or I will cry out and wake the house."

"They will think you dreaming, or out of your mind, and they will come and take the cup from you. Do let me put it away. Then you will go to sleep."

"I will not! I cannot trust you with it. You have destroyed my confidence in you. I may fall asleep, but if your hand comes within a foot of the cup, it will wake me. I shall sleep with my heart in the cup, and the least touch will wake me!"

"I wish you would let Andrew Ingram come to see you, sir."

"What's the matter with *him*?"

"Nothing's the matter with him, laird. But he helps everybody to do what is right."

"Conceited rascal! Do you take me for a maniac that you talk such foolery?"

His look was so wild, his old blue faded eyes gleamed with such a light of mingled fear and determination that Dawtie was almost sorry she had spoken. With trembling hands he drew the cup under his covers and lay still. If only the morning would come and bring George Crawford! *He* would take the cup back to its place, or hide it where he should know it safe and not far from him!

Dawtie sat motionless, and the old man fell into another feverish doze. She dared not stir lest he should start awake to defend his idol. She sat like a statue, moving only her eyes.

"What are you about, Dawtie?" he said at length. "You are after some mischief, you are so quiet."

"I was telling God how good you would be if he could get you to give up your odds and ends and take him instead."

"How dare you say such a thing, sitting there by my side! Are *you* to say to *him* that any sinner would be good if he would only do so and so with him! Tremble, girl, at the vengeance of the Almighty! How are you to presume to know what is best for another, and then tell *him* what you think!"

"We are told to make prayers and intercessions for all men,

and I was saying what I could for you."

The laird was silent, and the rest of the night passed quietly. His first words in the morning were, "Go and tell your mistress I want her."

When his daughter came, he told her to send for George Crawford. He was worse, he said, and wanted to see him.

Alexa thought it best to send Dawtie with the message by the next train. Dawtie did not relish the mission, for she had no faith in Crawford and did not think his influence on her master a good one. Nevertheless, she delivered her message in person, and then made haste back to Potlurg on the next train.

23 / The Watch

George came promptly and stayed with the laird a good while and had a long broken talk with him. When he left, Alexa came.

She thought her father seemed happier. George had put the cup away for him. Alexa sat by his bedside that night. She knew nothing of such a precious thing as the cup being in the house—in the very room—with them.

In the middle of the night, as she was arranging his pillows, the laird drew from under the covers the jeweled watch. She stared at it as he held it up to her, flashing in the light of the one candle. The old man was pleased at her surprise and evident admiration. She held out her hand for it. He gave it to her.

"That watch," he said, "is believed to have belonged to Ninon de Lenclos. It *may* have, but I doubt it myself. It is well known that she never took presents from her admirers, and she was too poor to have bought such a thing. Madame de Maintenon, however, or some one of her other friends, might have given it to her.—It will be yours one day—that is, if you marry the man I should like you to marry!"

"Dear Father, do not talk of marrying! I have all I want in you!" cried Alexa, inwardly feeling as if she hated George.

"Unfortunately, you will not have me much longer," returned her father. "I will say nothing more now, but I want you to consider what I have said."

Alexa put the watch in his hand.

"You do not suppose that a houseful of things like that would make any difference in whom I marry," she said.

159

He looked up at her sharply. A houseful!—what did she know?

It silenced him and he lay thinking. Surely the delight of lovely things must be in every woman's heart! Was not such a passion, developed or undeveloped, universal? Could a child of his *not* care for beautiful things?

"Ah," he said to himself, "she takes after her mother!"

A wall seemed to rise between him and his daughter. Alas! The things he loved and must one day yield would not be cherished by her! No tender regard would hover around them when he was gone! She would not be their protecting divinity to see that no harm came—

God in heaven! he thought suddenly—*she might*—no, the thought was too hideous. But now that he considered the possibility—yes, no doubt she *would* do it! He was sure she would sell them!

It seems the sole possible comfort of avarice, as it passes empty and hungry into the empty regions of the next life, is to make sure that the precious things it can no more see with eyes or handle with hands will somehow be yet left together. Hence, the rich leave to the rich, avoiding the man who most needs, or would best use, their money.

Is there a lurking notion in the man of many possessions, I wonder, that in the still watches of the night, when men sleep, he will return to look on what he leaves behind him? Does he forget the torture of seeing it at the command, in the enjoyment, of another—his will concerning this thing or that but a mockery?

As Alexa sat in the dim light by her brooding father, she found herself loathing the shining thing he had again replaced under the covers. She shrank from it as from a manacle the Devil had tried to slip on her wrist. The judicial assumption of society suddenly appeared in the emptiness of its arrogance. Marriage for the sake of *things!* Was she not a live soul, made for better than that!

The laird now and then cast a glance at her face and sighed. He gathered from it the conviction that she would be a cruel stepmother to his children, her mercy that of a loveless noncollector.

It should not be! He would do better for his precious ones than that!

Though he loved his daughter, he need not therefore sacrifice his last hopes where the sacrifice would meet with no acceptance. House and land should be hers, but not his jewels, his cups, his paintings, the prizes of his heart, the contents of his closet!

24 / The Will

George came again to see the laird the next day, and again had a long conference with him.

The laird told him that he had fully resolved to leave everything to his daughter, personal as well as real property, on the one condition that she should marry her cousin. If she would not, then the contents of his closet, with his library and certain articles specified, should pass to Crawford.

"And you must take care," said the laird, "if my death should come suddenly, that anything valuable in this room be taken into the closet before it is sealed up."

Shrinking as he did from the idea of death, the old man was yet able to talk about it in the interest of his possessions. It was as if he thought the sole consolation that his things could have, in the loss of their owner, was the continuation of their being together with each other in the heaven of his mammon-besotted imagination.

George responded heartily, showing a gratitude more genuine than fine. Every virtue partakes of the ground in which it is grown. He assured the laird that, valuable as was his contingent gift in itself, which no man could appreciate more than he, it would be far more valuable to him if it sealed his adoption as his son-in-law. He would rather owe the possession of the wonderful collection to the daughter than to the father! In either case the precious property would be held as for him, each thing as carefully tended as if it were by the laird's own eye and hand!

Whether it would at the moment have comforted the dying

man to be assured, as George might have assured him, that there would be nothing left of him to grieve at the loss of his idols—nothing left of him but a memory, to last so long as George and Alexa and one or two more should remain unburied, I cannot tell. It was in any case a dreary outlook for him.

Hope and faith and almost love had been sucked from his life by the insidious knotgrass, which had spread its white bloodless roots in all directions through soul and heart and mind, exhausting and choking in them everything of divinest origin. The weeds in George's heart were of another kind, neither better nor worse in themselves. The misery was that neither man was endeavoring to root them out.

The thief who is trying to be better is ages ahead of the most honorable man who is making no such effort. The one is alive, the other is dead and on the way to corruption.

Together they treated themselves to a gaze on the cup and the watch. Then George went to give directions to the laird's lawyer for the drawing up of Fordyce's new will.

The next day it was brought, read, signed by the laird, and his signature duly witnessed.

Being there and handy, Dawtie was made one of the witnesses. The laird trembled lest her fanaticism should break out in an appeal to the lawyer concerning the cup. He still could not understand that the cup was nothing to her, and that she did not imagine herself a setter right of wrongs, but knew herself her neighbor's keeper, one that had to try to deliver his soul from death. Had the cup come into her possession, she would have sent it back to the owner. But it was not worth her care that the Earl of Borland should cast his eyes when he would upon a valuable possession in a cabinet. The ache of her heart was in another direction!

Dawtie was very white as the laird signed his name. Where the others saw but a legal ceremony, she feared her loved master was assigning his soul to the Devil, as she had read of Dr. Faustus in the old ballad. Her master was gliding away into the dark, and no one to whom he had done a good turn with the mammon of unrighteousness was waiting to receive him into an everlasting habitation! She had needed no special reason to love her master any more than to love the chickens and the calves. She loved because something was there present to her to love. But he had always spoken kindly to her, and had been pleased with her attempts to serve him. And now he was going where she could do nothing for him—except pray, as her heart and Andrew had taught her. But alas! What were prayers where the man would not take the things prayed for! Nevertheless, all things *were* possible with God, and she *would* pray for him!

It was also with white face and with trembling hand that she signed her own name, for she felt as if she were giving him a push down the icy slope into the abyss.

But when the thing was done, the old man went quietly to sleep and dreamed of a radiant jewel more glorious than he had ever seen—ever within and yet ever just eluding his grasp.

25 / The End

The next day the laird seemed better, and Alexa again began to hope for his recovery.

But in the afternoon his pulse began to sink, and when Crawford came he could welcome him only with a smile and a vain effort to put out his hand. George bent down to him. At a sign from his eyes, the others left the room.

"I can't find it, George," he whispered.

"I put it away for you last night, you remember," answered George.

"No, you didn't. I had it in my hand a minute ago. But I fell into a doze, and it is gone! George, get it!—get it for me, or I shall go mad!"

George went and brought it to him.

"Thank you! Thank you! Now I remember! I thought I was in hell, and they took it from me!"

"Don't be afraid. Fall asleep when you feel inclined. I will keep my eye on the cup."

"You will not go away?"

"No. I will stay as long as you like. There is nothing to take me away. If I had thought you would be worse, I would not have left last night."

"I'm not worse! Don't you hear me speaking better?"

George nodded and attempted an assenting smile.

"I've thought about it, George," the laird went on, "and I am convinced the cup is a talisman! I am better all the time I hold it. It was because I let you put it away that I was worse last night.

If the chalice were not a talisman, how else could it have so nestled itself into my heart? I feel better, every time, the moment I take it in my hand. There is something more than common about that cup!—George, what if it should be the Holy Grail!"

He said the words with bated breath and a great white awe upon his countenance. His eyes were shining. His breath came and went rapidly. Slowly his aged cheeks flushed with two bright spots. He looked as if the joy of his life had come.

"What if it should be the Holy Grail!" he repeated, then fell asleep with the words on his lips.

As the evening deepened into night, he woke.

Crawford was sitting beside him. A change had come over the laird. He stared at George as if he could not make him out, closed his eyes, opened them, stared, and closed them again.

"Would you like me to call Alexa?" asked George.

"Call Dawtie. Go call Dawtie!" he replied.

George rose to go call her.

"Beware of her!" said the laird, with glazy eyes. "Beware of Dawtie!"

"How do you mean?" asked George.

"Beware of her," he repeated. "If she can get the cup, she will! She would take it from me now if she dared! She will steal it yet. Call Dawtie, call her!"

Alexa was in the drawing room, on the other side of the hall. George went and told her that her father wanted Dawtie.

"I will find her," she said, rising, but then turned and asked, "How does he seem now?"

"Rather worse," George answered.

"Are you going to be with him through the night?"

"I am. He insists on my staying with him," replied George, almost apologetically.

"Then you must have some supper," she returned. "We will go down and send Dawtie up."

He followed her to the kitchen. Dawtie was not there, but Alexa soon found her and sent her upstairs.

When the girl entered her master's room, she saw him lying motionless and white with the whiteness of death.

She got brandy and made him swallow some. As soon as he recovered a little, he began to talk wildly.

"Oh, Agnes!" he cried, "do not leave me. I'm not a bad man! I'm not what Dawtie calls me. I believe in the atonement. I put no trust in myself! My righteousness is as filthy rags. Take me with you. I *will* go with you! There! Slip that under your white robe—washed in the blood of the Lamb. That will hide it—with the rest of my sins. The unbelieving husband is sanctified by the believing wife. Take it! Take it! I should be lost in heaven without it! I can't see what I've got on, but it must be the robe of his righteousness, for I have none of my own. What should I be without it? It's all I've got! I couldn't bring away one other thing. And it's so cold to have but one thing on—I mean one thing in your hands! Do you say they will make me sell it? That would be worse than coming without it!"

He was talking to his wife—persuading her to smuggle the cup into heaven!

Dawtie's heart was about to break. She went on her knees behind the curtain of his bed and began to pray for him all she could. But after only a moment or two she was interrupted.

"Ah, I thought so!" said the voice of her master.

Dawtie opened her eyes—and there he was, holding back the curtain and looking round the edge of it with a face of eagerness, effort, and hate, as of one struggling to go, yet unable to break away.

"How could I go up to heaven with you praying against me like that!" he went on almost shrieking; "no doubt praying that he'll send both me and my cup to hell!"

Dawtie rose to her feet.

"You are a fiend!" he cried. "I *will* go with Agnes!"

He gave a cry and ceased. All was still.

In the kitchen they heard the cry and came running up.

They found Dawtie bending over her master with a scared

face. He seemed to have struck her, for one cheek was marked with red streaks across its whiteness.

"The Grail! The Sangreal!" he cried. "I have found it! I was bringing it home! She took it from me! She wants it to—"

His jaw fell, and he was dead.

Alexa threw herself beside the body. George would have raised her, but she resisted and lay motionless. He then stood beside her, watching for an opportunity to get the cup from under the covers of the bed that he might put it in the closet.

He ordered Dawtie to fetch water for her mistress, but Alexa told her she did not want any. Again George tried to raise her and at the same time to get his hands under the bedclothes to feel for the cup.

"He moved!" cried Alexa.

"Get some brandy," said George.

She rose and went to the table for the brandy. With the pretense of feeling the dead man's heart, George threw back the covers. He could find no cup. It must have gotten farther down by his feet. He would wait.

Alexa lifted her father's head on her arm, but it was plain that brandy could not help. Whatever movement there was had been only imagined.

She went and sat on a chair away from the bed, hopeless and exhausted. George lifted the covers from the foot of the bed, then from the farther side, and then from the nearer—all without attracting her attention.

But still the cup was nowhere to be seen. He put his hand under the body, but the cup was not there! He could not continue his search. He had to leave the room that Dawtie and Meg might prepare the master for burial. Alexa rose and went to her chamber.

A moment after she was gone George returned, called Meg to the door and said, "There must be a brass cup in the bed somewhere. I brought it to amuse him. He was fond of odd things, you know. If you should find it—"

"I will take care of it," answered Meg, and turned from him

curtly. George felt that he had not a friend in the house, and that he must leave things as they were. To continue the search himself or ask too many questions might only arouse suspicions. The door of the closet was locked, and he could not go again into the death chamber to take the laird's keys from the head of the bed. He knew that the two women would not let him.

It had been an oversight not to secure them. He was glad the watch was safe, that he had put it in the closet earlier. But that hardly mattered when the valuable cup was missing!

He went to the stable, got his horse, and rode home in the still gray of a midsummer night.

The stillness and the night seemed to be thinking to each other. George had little imagination, but what he did have now awakened in him as he rode slowly along. Step for step the old man seemed to be following him—on silent churchyard feet, through the eerie whiteness of the night. There was neither cloud nor moon, only stars above and around, and a great cold crack in the northeast.

The laird was crying after him in a voice the old man could not make George hear! Was he struggling to warn Crawford not to come into like condemnation? The voice seemed trying to say, "I know now! I know now! I would not believe, but I know now! Give back the cup! Give it back!"

George did not let himself believe that there was "anything" there. It was but a vague movement in that commonplace, unmysterious region—his mind! He heard nothing, positively nothing, with his ears. Therefore, there was nothing! There could be no proof, no evidence, no actual sound—therefore had been no words!

It was indeed somehow as if one were saying the words, but in reality they came only as a thought rising, continually rising, in his mind. It was but a thought-sound and no speech: "I know now! I know now! Give back the cup! Give it back!"

He did not ask himself how the thought came, but cast it away as an insignificant thing, a thought. Nonetheless, he found himself answering it: "I can't give it back. I can't find it. Where did you put it? You must have taken it with you!"

"Rubbish!" he said to himself, coming back to his "right mind," as he would have put it. "Dawtie took it, of course! The old fellow warned me to beware of her. Nobody but her was in the room when we ran in and found him at the point of death."

He reviewed in his mind all that had taken place. The laird had the cup when George left him to call Dawtie, and when he and Alexa came in just a few minutes later, the cup was nowhere to be found!

He was convinced the girl had secured it somewhere—in obedience, no doubt, to the instructions of that farmer fellow she was said to admire, her spiritual director the laird said, ambitious to do justice and curry the favor of the earl by restoring it again into his hand! She had grabbed the cup when the opportunity presented itself, and was now waiting for a chance to sneak it out of the house! If she hadn't already!

But he could do nothing till the will was read.

Was it possible Alexa had put it away? he wondered. No, she had not had the opportunity. He had been with her when she came into the room.

26 / George and the Golden Goblet_____

With slow-pacing shadows, the hot hours crept across the heath and the house and the dead, and carried the living with them in their invisible current. There is no tide in time. It is a steady current in one direction, never returning. Happy are they whom it bears inward to the center of things. Alas for those whom it carries outward to the flaming walls of creation!

The poor old laird, who, with all his refinement, all his education, all his interest in philology, prosody, history, and reliquial humanity, had become the slave of a goblet, had left it behind him, had faced the empty universe empty-handed, and vanished with a shadow-goblet in his heart. The eyes that gloated over the gems had gone to help the grass grow.

But the will of the dead remained for a time to trouble the living, for it put his daughter in a painful predicament. Until Crawford's property was removed from the house, it would give him constant opportunity of prosecuting the suit that Alexa had reason to think he intended to resume, and the thought had become to her insupportable.

Great was Alexa's astonishment when she learned to what the door of the study led, and what a multitude of curious and valuable things were there of whose presence in the house she had never dreamed. She would gladly have had them for herself, and it pained her to the heart to think of the disappointment of the poor ghost when he saw, if he could, his treasured hoard emptied out of its hidden and safe abode. For even if George should magnanimously protest that he did not care for the things enough to claim them and beg for them to remain where they were—an unlikely enough possibility!—she could not grant his request, for it would be to accept them from him. She would not marry him and have the treasures that way, nor would she receive them as a gift from his hand. Out of Potlurg they were destined to go! And even had her father left them to her, she would have kept them as carefully as even he could desire—but she would never have allowed them to remain shut up where they could not give pleasure to others.

Alexa was growing to care more about the truth. She was gradually coming to see that much of what she had taken for a more liberal creed was but the same falsehoods in weaker forms of the constricting religion from which her mind had rebelled. In Andrew she saw what was infinitely higher and more than the religion of various doctrines and prohibitions of her ancestors—namely, the denial of his very self, and the reception of God instead. She was beginning to realize that she had been, even with all her supposed progress, only a recipient of the traditions of the elders. Yet there must be a deeper something . . . somewhere—the *real* religion that would satisfy heart and soul!

Her eyes were gradually opening, but she did not yet see that the will of God lay in another direction altogether than the heart-iest reception of dogma and creed and doctrine, no matter how right they be!—that God was too great and too generous to care about anything except righteousness, and only wanted us to be good children!

She pondered much about her father, and would find herself praying for him, careless of what she had read in God's Word about the permanency of the spiritual state of the dead. She could not blind herself to what she knew. He had not been a bad man, as men count badness. But could she in common sense think him a glorified saint, singing in white robes? The polite, kind old man, her own father! Righteous he could never be called! But how bad was he, on the other hand? Could she believe him tormenting in flames forever? If so, what kind of a religion would require her to believe he was in torment, and at the same time expect her to rejoice in the Lord always?

She longed for something positive to believe, something in accordance with which her feelings might agree. She was still on the outlook for definite intellectual formulae to hold. Like so many seeming Christians, she could not divorce her mind from thinking of belief as a framework of viewpoints—social, political, philosophical, and theoretical, none of which the Lord had anywhere in his mind when he said, "Repent and *believe* in the gospel." True belief consists in no cognitive convictions, no matter how pious, no matter how biblically correct, but rather in *life* as it is *lived!*

Alexa's interaction with Andrew had as yet failed to open her eyes to the fact that the faith required of us is faith in a person, not in the truest of statements concerning anything, even concerning Him, for some do not discern his truth correctly. Neither was she yet alive to the fact that faith in the living One, the very essence of it, consists in obedience to him. A man can obey before he is intellectually sure; and except he obey the command he knows to be right, wherever it may come from, he will never be sure. To find the truth, a man or woman must be true.

She found, from all her thinking, that she greatly desired another talk with Andrew.

George persuaded himself that in the midst of her grief, Alexa's former feeling toward him would reassert itself. He was also confident that she would be loath to part with her father's wonderful collection, and thus he waited for the effect of the will. After the reading of it, he had gone away directly, so that his presence would not add to the irritation which he concluded, not without reason, her father's stipulations were likely to cause her, even in the midst of her sorrow. But at the end of a week he wrote, saying that he felt it his duty, if only in gratitude to his friend the laird, to find out for himself what attention the valuable things he had left him might require. He assured Alexa that he had done nothing to influence her father in the matter, and much regretted the awkward position in which his will had placed both her and him. At the same time, it was not unnatural that he should wish such precious objects to be possessed by one who would care for them as he himself had cared for them. He hoped, therefore, that she would allow him access to her father's rooms. He would not, she might rest assured, intrude himself upon her sorrow, though he would be compelled to ask her before long whether he might hope that her father's wish would have any influence in reviving the favor which had once been the joy of his life.

Alexa saw that if she consented to see him, he would take it as a permission to press his claim, and the very thought of marrying him was further from her mind than ever. Therefore she wrote him a stiff letter, telling him the house was at his service, but he must excuse her if she did not see him.

The next morning brought him early to Potlurg. The cause of his haste was his uneasiness about the chalice.

Old Meg opened the door to him, and he followed her straight into the drawing room. Alexa was there and was far from expecting him. But annoyed at his appearance as she was, she found his manner and behavior less unpleasant than usual. He was gentle and self-restrained, assuming no familiarity beyond that of a distant relative, and gave the impression of having come against his will and only from a sense of duty.

"Did you not receive my note?" she asked. He had hoped, he said, to save her the trouble of writing. She handed him her father's bunch of keys, then left the room.

George went straight to the laird's closet, and having spent an hour in it, again sought Alexa. The jeweled watch was in his hand.

"I feel more pleasure, Alexa," he said, "in begging you to accept this trinket since it was the last addition to your dear father's collection. I myself had the good fortune to please him with it a few days before his death."

"No, thank you, George," returned Alexa. "It is beautiful—my father showed it to me—but I cannot take it."

"I was thinking more of you than him when I purchased it, Alexa. You know why I could not offer it to you."

"The same reason still exists."

"I am sorry to have to force myself upon your attention, but—

"Dawtie!" cried Alexa.

Dawtie came running.

"Wait there a minute, Dawtie. I will speak to you presently," said her mistress.

George rose. He had laid the watch on the table and seemed to have forgotten it.

"Please take the watch with you," said Alexa.

"Certainly, if you wish!" he answered.

"And my father's keys too," she added.

"Will you not be kind enough to take charge of them?"

"I would rather not be accountable for anything under them."

"I cannot help regretting," said George, "that your honored father should have thought fit to lay this burden of possession upon me."

Alexa made no answer.

"I comforted myself with the hope that you would feel them as much your own as ever!" he resumed, in a tone of disappointment and dejection.

"I did not know of their existence before I knew they were never to be mine."

"Never, Alexa?"

"Never."

George walked to the door, but there turned, and said, "By the way, you know that cup your father was so fond of?"

"No."

"That gold cup, set with stones?"

"I saw something in his hands once, in bed. That might have been a cup."

"It is a thing of great value—of pure gold, and every stone in it a gem."

"Indeed!" returned Alexa with marked indifference.

"Yes. It was the work of the famous Benvenuto Cellini, made for Pope Clement the seventh, for his communion chalice. Your father priced it at three thousand pounds. In his last moments, when his mind was wandering, he fancied it the Holy Grail. He had it in the bed with him when he died—that I know."

"And it is missing?"

"Perhaps Dawtie could tell us what has become of it. She was with the laird in his last moments."

Dawtie, who had stood aside to let him pass to the open door, looked up with a flash in her eyes, but said nothing.

"Have you seen the cup, Dawtie?" asked her mistress.

"No, ma'am."

"Do you know it?"

"Very well, ma'am."

"But you don't know what has become of it?"

"No, ma'am. I know nothing about it."

"Take care, Dawtie!" said George. "This is a matter that will have to be searched into."

"When did you last see it, Dawtie?" inquired Alexa.

"The very day the master died, ma'am. He was looking at it, but when I saw it, he covered it up inside the bed."

"And you have not seen it since?"

"No, ma'am."

"And you do not know where it is?" asked George.

"No, sir. How should I?"

"You have never touched it?"

"I cannot say that. I brought it to him from his closet. He sent me for it."

"What do you think may have become of it?"

"I don't know."

"Would you allow me to make a thorough search in the place where it was last seen?" asked George, turning to his cousin.

"By all means. Dawtie, go and help Mr. Crawford look for it."

"It can't be there, ma'am. We've had the carpet up, and the

floor scrubbed. There's not a hole or corner we haven't been into—and that was yesterday."

"We must find it!" said George.

"It must be in the house, sir," replied Dawtie.

But George more than half doubted it. He cast her a quick glance, but then went on as if musing to himself.

"I do believe the laird would rather have lost his whole collection," he said.

"Indeed, sir," returned Dawtie, "I think you are right."

"Then you have talked to him about it?"

"Yes, I have sir," answered Dawtie, sorry she had brought up the question.

"And you know the worth of the thing?"

"Yes, sir; that is, I don't know how much it was worth, but I should say pounds and pounds."

"Then, Dawtie, I must ask you again, *where is it?*"

"I know nothing about it, sir. I wish I did."

"Why do you wish you did?"

"Because—" began Dawtie, then stopped short. She shrank from impugning the honesty of the dead man—especially in the presence of his daughter. But to go on would be to say she thought the laird as good as a thief as long as he possessed the cup knowing it was not rightfully his.

"It looks a little fishy, doesn't it, Dawtie? Why not speak straight out? Perhaps you would not mind searching Meg's trunk for me. She may have taken it for a bit of old brass, you know."

"I will answer for my servants, Mr. Crawford!" said Alexa. "I will not have old Meg's box searched!"

"We must get rid of any suspicion," replied George.

"I have none," returned Alexa.

George was silent.

"I will ask Meg, if you like, sir," said Dawtie. "But I am sure it will be no use. A servant in this house soon learns not to go by the look of things."

"When did you first see the goblet?" persisted George. "What do you know about it?"

"I know very little about it."

"It is plain you know more than you care to tell. If you will not answer me, you will have to answer a judge."

"Then I will answer a judge," said Dawtie, beginning to grow a little angry.

"You had better answer me, Dawtie! It will be easier for you. What do you know about the cup?"

"I know it was not master's, and is not yours—really and truly."

"What could have put such a lie in your head!"

"If it be a lie, it is told in plain print."

"Where?"

But Dawtie judged it time to stop. She realized that she would not have said so much had she not been angry.

"Sir," she answered, "you have been asking me questions all this time, and I have been answering them. Now it is your turn to answer me one."

"If I see it proper."

"Did my old master tell you the history of the cup?"

"I do not choose to answer the question."

"Very well, sir."

Dawtie turned to leave the room.

"Stop!" cried Crawford. "I am not done with you yet, my girl! You have not told me what you meant when you said the cup did not belong to the laird!"

"I do not choose to answer the question," said Dawtie.

"Then you shall answer it to a judge!"

"I will be glad to do so," she replied, and stood where she was.

Crawford left the room.

He rode home in a rage. Dawtie went about her work with a red flush on each cheek, indignant at the man's rudeness, but praying to God to take her heart in his hand and cool the fever of it.

The words rose in her mind: "It must be that offenses come, but woe unto that man by whom they come!" She was at once filled with pity for the man who could side with the wrong, and want everything his own way. Sooner or later, confession must be his portion, for the Lord said, "There is nothing covered that shall not be revealed, neither hid that shall not be known."

George felt that he had not carried himself in the most dignified way, and knew that his last chance with Alexa was gone. At the same time, he felt the situation unendurable, and set about immediately to remove his property. He wrote to Alexa that he could no longer doubt it her wish to be rid of the collection and able to use the room for other purposes. It was desirable also, he said, that a thorough search should be made in those rooms before he placed the matter of the missing cup in the hands of the magistrates.

Dawtie's last words had sufficed to remove any lingering doubt as to what had become of the chalice. It did not occur to him that one so anxious to do the justice of restoration would hardly be capable of telling lies, of defiling her soul that a bit of property might be recovered. He took it for granted that she meant to be liberally rewarded by the earl for returning the cup to him.

George would have ill understood the distinction Dawtie made—that the body of the cup *might* belong to him, but the soul of the cup *did* belong to another; or her assertion that where the soul was, there the body ought to be.

George suspected, and grew convinced that Alexa was a party to the abduction of the cup. She had, he said to himself, begun to share in the extravagant notions of a group of pietists whose leader was that detestable fellow Ingram. Alexa was attached to Dawtie, and Dawtie was one of them. He believed Alexa would do anything to spite him. To bring trouble on Dawtie would serve to punish her mistress, and the pious farmer too!

27 / The Prosecution

As soon as Crawford managed to get the laird's former things away from Potlurg, satisfied that the cup was nowhere among them, he made a statement of the case to a magistrate he knew. Aware of the man's views, he so represented it as the outcome of the hypocrisy of pietism, that the judge, hating everything called fanatical, at once granted him a warrant to apprehend Dawtie on the charge of theft.

It was a terrible shock. Alexa cried out with indignation when she read the paper handed to her by the man serving as the agent for George's dirty work. Dawtie turned white when Alexa found her and broke the news, then her face grew red, but she uttered never a word.

"Dawtie," said her mistress, "tell me what you know about the cup. You do know something that you have not told me, do you not?"

"I do, ma'am, but I will not tell it unless I am forced to."

"That you are going to be, my poor girl! I am very sorry, for I am perfectly sure you have done nothing you know to be wrong. But I do not see what I can do to help you."

"I have done nothing that you or anybody would think wrong, ma'am," replied Dawtie.

She put on her Sunday frock and then went downstairs to go with the policeman. Alexa was at the door waiting, to Dawtie's joy, ready to accompany her. They had two miles or more to walk, but that was nothing to either. The policeman took her straight to the judge, where they found George awaiting their arrival.

Questioned by the magistrate, not unkindly, for her mistress was there, Dawtie told everything—how first she had happened upon the picture and history of the cup in the book, and then saw the cup itself in her master's hands.

Crawford told how the laird had warned him against Dawtie, giving him to understand that she had been seized with a passion for the goblet such that she would peril her soul to possess it, and that he dared not let her know where it was.

"Sir," said Dawtie in response, "he couldn't have distrusted me like that, for he gave me his keys and sent me to fetch the cup when he was too ill to get it himself."

"If that be true, your worship," said Crawford, "it does not alter the fact that the cup was in the hands of the old man when I left him and she went to him, and from that moment it has not been seen."

"Did he have it when you went to him?" asked the judge.

"I didn't see it, sir. He was in a kind of faint when I got up to his room."

Crawford said that, hearing a cry, he ran up the stairs again, and found the old man at the point of death, with just strength to cry out before he died that Dawtie had taken the cup from him. Dawtie was leaning over him, but he had not imagined the accusation more than the delirious fancy of a dying man, till it appeared that the cup was not to be found.

The magistrate then made out a paper committing Dawtie over for trial.

He remarked that she might have been misled by a false notion of duty. He had been informed that she belonged to a sect claiming the right to think for themselves on the profoundest mysteries—and here was the result!

There was not a man in Scotland less capable of knowing what any woman was thinking, or more incapable of doubting his own insight.

Doubtless, he went on, she had superstitiously regarded the cup as exercising a satanic influence on the mind of her master.

But even if she confessed to the theft now and restored the goblet, he must make an example of one whose fanaticism would set wrong right after the notions of an illiterate sect, and not according to the laws of the land. He had no choice but to send the case to be tried by a jury. If she convinced the twelve men composing the jury of the innocence she protested, she would then be a free woman—but not before!

Dawtie stood very white all the time he was speaking, and her lips every now and then quivered as if she were going to cry, but she did not. Alexa offered bail, but his worship would not accept it. His righteous soul was too indignant. She would await the trial in jail, he said.

Alexa went to Dawtie and kissed her, and together they followed the policeman to the door, where Dawtie was to get into a carriage with him and be driven to the county town, there to lie awaiting her trial.

The news had spread so fast that as they came out of the courtroom, up came Andrew. At the sight of him Dawtie gently laughed, like a pleased child. The policeman, who, like many present, had been prejudiced in her favor by her looks and behavior dropped back a step, and she walked between her mistress and Andrew to the carriage.

"Dawtie!" said Andrew.

"Oh, Andrew! Here I am on my road to prison. I didn't think God would let them do it to me! I feel like he's forgotten me!"

"God hasn't forgotten you, Dawtie," replied Andrew. "To forget would be for him to be God no longer. He's still all about you and in you, Dawtie, and this has come to you just to let you know that he is. He raised you up just to spend his glory upon!"

"But it's a sore trial, Andrew, hearing them lie about me!"

"Did Jesus deserve what he got, Dawtie?"

"Not a bit, Andrew!"

"Do you think God had forgotten him?"

"Maybe he thought it just for a minute."

"Well, you have now thought it just for a minute, and you must think it no more."

"But God couldn't forget *him*, Andrew. He got what happened to him all from doing his will!"

"Evil may come upon us from other causes than doing the will of God. But from whatever cause it comes, the thing we have to see to is that through it all, we do the will of God."

"What's his will now, Andrew?"

"That you take it quietly. Shall not the Father do with his own child what he will! Can he not shift it from one arm to the other, even though the child may cry? He has you in his arms, Dawtie! It's all right!"

"Though he slay me, yet will I trust him. Is that what you would have me remember, Andrew, like you've said to me before?" said Dawtie with a faint smile.

"Aye! We can *always* trust him!"

Dawtie raised her head. The color had come back to her face, and her lip had stopped trembling. She walked on steadily to where the carriage was waiting her. She bade her mistress goodbye, then turned to Andrew and said, "Goodbye, Andrew. I am not afraid."

"I am going with you, Dawtie," said Andrew.

"No, sir, you can't do that!" said the policeman; "—at least I can't let you go in the carriage."

"No, no, Andrew," said Dawtie. "I am well able to go alone. God will do with me as he pleases."

"I am going with you," said Alexa, "if the policeman will let me."

"Oh, yes, ma'am. A lady's different, you see!"

"I don't think you should, ma'am," said Dawtie. "It's a long way!"

"I am going," returned her mistress decisively.

"God bless you!" said Andrew to Alexa. He then took Dawtie's hand and gave it a final squeeze as the two ladies climbed up.

As they drove off, Andrew standing watching them go, Alexa was quietly pondering many things. But for the moment Dawtie's fate was not uppermost in her mind. She had heard everything that had passed between Andrew and Dawtie, and a new light had broken upon her. "So that is what they think God is like!" she said to herself. "You can go up close to him whenever you please! How wonderful! If only it might be true!"

28 / A Talk at Potlurg

It would be three weeks before Dawtie's trial. The house of Potlurg was searched by the police from garret to cellar, but in vain. The cup was not found.

As soon as they gave up searching, Alexa had the old door of the laird's closet, discernible enough on the inside, reopened, and the room cleaned. Almost unfurnished as it was, she made of it her sitting parlor. But often her work or her book would lie on her lap, and she would find herself praying for the dear father for whom she could do nothing else now, but for whom she might have done so much more had she been like Dawtie. She lamented more than once that her servant had cared for her father more than she.

As she sat there one morning alone, brooding a little, thinking a little, reading a little, and praying through it all, Meg appeared and said that Master Andrew was at the door requesting to see her.

He had called more than once during the last year or two to see Dawtie, but never before had he asked to see her mistress.

Alexa found herself unaccountably agitated. When he walked into the room, however, she was able to receive him quietly. He came, he said, to ask when she had last seen Dawtie. He himself would have gone to see her, but his father was ailing and he had double work to do on the farm, which allowed him no time to get to the county town.

Alexa told him she had been to visit the girl the day before, and had found her a little pale, and, she feared, rather troubled.

186

Dawtie said she would trust God to the last, but confessed herself assailed by doubts.

"I said to her," continued Alexa, " 'Be sure, Dawtie, God will make your innocence known one day.' She answered, 'Of course, ma'am, there is nothing hidden that shall not be known; but I am not worried about that.' 'But surely,' I said, 'you care that people should understand that you are not a thief, Dawtie!' 'Yes,' she answered, 'but that does not trouble me so much. I only want to be downright sure that God is looking after me all the time. I am willing to sit in prison till I die if he pleases. I only want to know that God has not left me. That is what makes this an ordeal, when I begin to think he has! I can't bear it when I begin to doubt his goodness!' "

"You see, ma'am, it comes to this," said Andrew: "It is God Dawtie cares about, not herself, and not what people think of her. If God is all right, Dawtie is all right. The very fear he may have left her is faith."

"What would you have said to her, Mr. Ingram?"

"I would have reminded her that Jesus was perfectly content with his Father, that he knew what was coming on himself, and never doubted him—just gloried that his Father was what he knew him to be."

"I see . . . But what did you mean when you said that Dawtie's very fear was faith?"

"Think about it, ma'am. People that only care to be saved, that is, not to be punished for their sins, are anxious only about themselves, not about God and his glory at all. They talk about the glory of God, but they make it consist in pure selfishness! According to them, he seeks everything for himself, which is dead against the truth of God, a diabolical slander of his true character. It does not trouble them to believe such things about God. They do not even desire that God should not be like that; they only want to escape him. They dare not say that God will not do this or that, however clear it be that it would not be fair or just, for they live in mortal terror of contradicting the Bible. They make more of the Bible than of God. They superficially examine its statutes for a system of laws more than they search out its *life* for God's loving character. Thus, they fail to find the truth of the Bible, and in so doing they accept things concerning God to which they think the Bible points, but which are not in the Bible at all, and are in fact great insults to him! The letter of the law pleases their intellects; the spirit of God's essential being they never let into their hearts."

"And Dawtie?"

"Dawtie never thinks about saving her soul, any more than she worries whether people think she is a thief. She has no fear either for her soul or for her reputation. She is only anxious about God and the glory of his character. If she did not love God, the doubts in her mind would not be there. The doubts in her mind point to a God of another character than she knows him to be. Free Dawtie from unsureness about God, and she has no fear left. All is well, in the prison or on the throne of God, if he only be what she thinks he is."

"But how can such doubts arise in one who loves God as Dawtie does?"

"Doubt and faith often go hand in hand. Did not Jesus honor the man who said, 'I believe, help my unbelief'? God's children are not yet God's men and women."

Alexa pondered his words a moment. Then she said, "I do not think you would find many church people agreeing with you on the nature of the God whose character you so lovingly represent."

"I am sure you are right," replied Andrew. "The God that many people say they believe in is a God not worth believing in, a God that ought not to be believed in. A God like that could not make a woman like Dawtie anxious about his character and his trustworthiness. If God is not like Jesus, it would mean nothing to Dawtie even though proved innocent before the whole world. If God be not altogether good, there is nothing left to live for. But to know that there is a perfect God, one for us to love with all the power of love of which we are capable—to know *that* is worth going out of existence for! And to know that God *himself*— to know him as his friend!—must make every throb of conscious- ness a divine ecstasy!''

Andrew's heart was full, and out of its fullness he spoke. Never before in the presence of Alexa had he been able to speak as he felt. Never before had he had any impulse to speak as now. As soon would he have gone out to sow seed on a bare rock as to sow words of spirit and life in her ears. But the seed was not now being sown on rock, for there was now soil where once had been stone. Thus, when the seed struck, it began to send forth roots.

"I am beginning to understand you," she said. "Will you forgive me? I have been very self-confident and conceited. What a mercy from God that things are not as I thought they were."

"Men's hearts shall be full of bliss because they have found their Father," quoted Andrew in response, "and he is what he is, and they are going home to him."

Then he rose.

"You will come to see me again soon—will you not?" said Alexa.

"As often as you please. I am your servant."

"Then, please come tomorrow."

Andrew returned to Potlurg the next day, and the day after, and the day after that—nearly every day while Dawtie was await- ing her trial.

Almost every morning Alexa went by train to visit Dawtie. The news she brought, Andrew would then carry to the girl's parents. Andrew wanted to go see her, but Dawtie expressed an unwillingness to see him. He had enough trouble with her already, she said.

Andrew could not for the life of him understand her refusal.

29 / A Great Offering

Two days before the trial, Andrew was with Alexa in her parlor. It was a cool autumn evening, and she suggested they should take a walk out on the heath, which came close up to the back of the house.

When they reached the top of the hill, a cold wind was blowing. Full of care for old and young, man and woman, Andrew made Alexa draw her shawl closer about her throat, where he pinned it for her with his rough ploughman hands. She saw, felt, and noted his hands. An admiration for them awoke in her, and before she knew it she was gazing up in his face with such a light in her eyes that Andrew found himself embarrassed and let his eyes fall. Moved by that sense of class-superiority that has no place in the kingdom of heaven, she attributed his modesty to self-depreciation. The conviction rose in her that there is a magnanimity demanding the sacrifice, not merely of conventional dignity, but of conventional propriety. She felt that a great lady to be more than great, she must stoop, that it was her part to make the approach which, between equals of the same class, would have been the part of the man. The patroness *must* do what the woman might not. This man was worthy of any woman, be she a farmer's sister or daughter of an earl!

"Andrew," she said, "I am going to do an unusual thing, but you are not like other men, and you will not misunderstand. I know you now—know that you are as far above other men as the clouds are above the heath on this moor."

"Oh no, ma'am!" protested Andrew. "I am not a bit—"

"Hear me out, Andrew," she interrupted, then paused a little.

"Tell me," she resumed in a moment, "ought we not to love most strongly the best we know?"

"Surely," he answered, uncomfortable, but not anticipating what was on the way.

"Andrew, you are the best I know! There, I have said it—I do not care what the world thinks. You are more to me than the opinion of the world! If you will take me, I am yours."

She looked him in the face with the feeling that she had done a brave and a right thing.

Andrew stood stock-still.

"*Me*, ma'am!" he gasped, incredulous, growing pale—then gradually red as a foggy sun.

"You, Andrew! You have helped me understand so many things! I cannot imagine going on in life without you to continue to guide me."

"It's a Godlike thing you have done," he said slowly. "But—but I cannot make the return it deserves. From the heart of my heart I thank you. But—"

His voice trembled.

"—I can say no more," he added, and was then silent. Alexa heard a stifled sob. He had turned away to conceal his emotion.

And now indeed came greatness to the front. Instead of drawing herself up with the bitter pride of a woman whose love has been scorned, Alexa behaved divinely. She went close to Andrew, laid her hand on his arm, and said, "Forgive me, Andrew. I made a mistake. I had no right to make it."

"Please, ma'am," faltered Andrew, "think nothing of it. It is only that—"

"Say nothing more, Andrew," she interrupted again. "My pain will pass."

"I am sorry, ma'am."

"Will you not at least agree to call me by my name?"

Andrew looked up and smiled.

"Very well," he said. "I am sorry . . . Alexa."

"Do not be grieved over this, I beg you. You are in no way to blame. Let us continue to be friends."

"Thank you," responded Andrew, in a tone of deepest gratitude. Neither said a word more. They walked side by side back to the house.

As they went, Alexa said to herself, "At least I have been refused by a man worthy of honor. I may have been mistaken to do what I did, but I made no mistake in *him*."

When they reached the door, she stopped. Andrew took off his hat and said, holding it in his hand as he spoke, "Good night, Alexa! You *will* send for me if you want to talk?"

"I will! Good night, Andrew!" replied Alexa, then turned to go inside with a strange weight on her heart.

She went straight to her room, shut herself in, and wept sorely, but not bitterly. The next day old Meg, at least, saw no change in her.

Humbled by the experience, Andrew said to himself as he walked home, "I will be her servant always."

30 / Another Offering_____

The next evening, just before the trial, Andrew presented himself at the prison and was admitted. When he and Dawtie met, she came up to him, held out her hand, and said, "Thank you for coming, Andrew!"

"How are you, Dawtie?"

"Well enough. God is with me, but sometimes it is hard to feel him."

"I cannot always see God's eyes looking at me, Dawtie, or feel him in my heart. But when we are ready to do what he wants us to do, we can know he is with us."

"Oh, Andrew, I wish I could be sure!"

"Even if he showed himself to us in person, the sight of him would make us believe in him without knowing him. What kind of faith would that be for him or for us! We must *know* him! And we come to know him by trusting him. It is hard upon God that his own children will not trust him, when his perfect love is our perfect safety. But one day we shall know and trust him, Dawtie. When we do, there will be no fear, no doubt. We shall run straight home!—Dawtie, shall we go together?"

"Yes, surely, Andrew! I'm ready to do whatever you tell me."

"No, Dawtie. You must never do something just because I tell you, except you think it right."

"Yes, I know. But I am sure I should think it right."

A pause followed. Andrew glanced away under Dawtie's gaze. She did not understand his silence or his apparent uneasiness. Still she looked into his face, waiting for him to speak again.

Finally he looked up, and once more sought her eyes with his.

"We've been of one mind for a long time now, Dawtie," he said at length.

"Since long before I had any mind of my own!" replied Dawtie.

"Then let us be of one heart too, Dawtie!"

She was so accustomed to hearing Andrew speak in figures that sometimes she looked through and beyond his words, trying to find some hidden meaning. She did so now, and seeing nothing, stood perplexed.

"Won't you, Dawtie?" said Andrew, holding out his hands.

"I don't understand you, Andrew."

"You heavenly idiot!" cried Andrew. "Will you be my wife, or won't you?"

Dawtie threw her shapely arms above her head—straight up. Her head fell back and she seemed to gaze above her into the unseen. Then she gave a gasp, her arms dropped to her sides, and she would have fallen had not Andrew taken her.

"Andrew!" she sighed, and was still in his arms.

"Will you, Dawtie?" he whispered.

"Wait," she murmured.

"I won't wait."

"Wait till you hear what they say in the morning."

"Dawtie! What do I care what they say! Are you not the Lord's clean little lamb? If you care for what any man thinks of you but the Lord himself, you're not one of his."

"But, Andrew, it won't do to say of your father's son that he took his wife from the jail!"

"Indeed, what else should they say. That's why I came! Would you have me ashamed of one of God's elect—a lady of the Lord's own court?"

"Eh, but I'm afraid it's all from the compassion in your heart! You would make up to me for the disgrace I'm in. You could well do without me!"

"I won't say," returned Andrew, "that I couldn't live without you, for that would be to say I wasn't worth offering you, and it would be to deny him that made you and me for one another. But I would have a sore time! I'll tell the minister to be ready the minute the Lord opens your prison door."

The next moment, in came the governor with his wife. They had visited Dawtie several times before and had grown very interested in her. Andrew recognized the official.

"Sir and ma'am," said Andrew, "will you be willing to witness that this woman is my wife?"

"It's Master Andrew Ingram of the Knowe," explained Dawtie to her two friends. "He wants me to marry him."

"I want her to go before the court tomorrow as my wife," said Andrew. "She would have me wait till the jury gives their verdict. Then it would be for the jury to decide whether to give me my wife or not! As if I didn't know her!"

"You won't have him, I see," commented the governor's wife, turning to Dawtie.

"Have him!" cried Dawtie. "I would have him if there were but the head of him!"

"Then you *are* husband and wife," returned the governor. "Only you should have the thing done properly by a minister."

"I'll see to that, sir," said Andrew, "the moment Dawtie is out of this place!"

"Come," beckoned the governor to his wife, "we must let them have a few minutes alone together."

"There!" exclaimed Andrew when the door closed, "you're my wife now, Dawtie! Let them acquit you or condemn you. It's you and me now, whatever comes!"

Dawtie broke into a flood of tears—an experience all but new to her—and found it did her good. She smiled as she wiped her eyes.

"Well, Andrew," she said, "if the Lord hasn't appeared in his own likeness to deliver me, he's done the next best thing."

"The Lord never does the next best thing," replied Andrew. "The thing he does is always better than the thing he does not.

The *best* thing, when a person's not ready for it, would be the *worst* to give him—or anyway, not the thing for the Father of Lights to give! Shortbread might be worse for a half-starved child than a stone. But the minute it's fit for us to look upon the face of the Son of Man, our own God-born brother, we'll see him, Dawtie! Heart can't imagine what it'll be like!—And now, Dawtie, will you tell me why you wouldn't let me come to see you before?"

"I will, Andrew. You see, it's like this—I was no sooner left to myself in this prison than I found myself thinking about *you*—you first, and not the Lord. I said to myself, 'I'm leaning on Andrew and not on the Father.' I saw that I was breaking away from him that was nearest me, and trusting one that was farther away. So I said to myself that I would meet my fate with the Lord alone, and wouldn't have you come between him and me!"

Andrew took her in his arms.

"Thank you for telling me, Dawtie!" he said. "Eh, but I *am* content! And you thought you had no faith!"

Dawtie smiled up at him.

"Now, good night!" he added. "You must get to bed and grow stout in heart for tomorrow."

31 / After the Verdict_____

Andrew obtained permission to stand near the prisoner at the trial. The counsel for the prosecution did all he could, and the counsel for the defense seemingly not much—but at least the judge appointed to hear the case summed it up with the greatest impartiality.

Dawtie's calmness and simplicity, her confidence without any self-assertion, had its influence on the jury. And though they could not state categorically that she was "innocent," they rendered the next best verdict with the words—*Not Proven,* so that Dawtie was discharged.

Alexa had a carriage ready to take her home. As Dawtie went to it, Andrew whispered to her, "You'll be over to see your old folk tonight?"

"Yes, Andrew. I'm sure the mistress will let me."

"Don't say a word to her of our marriage. I want to tell her myself. You will find me at the croft when you come, and I will go back with you."

In the evening Dawtie came, bringing with her the message that her mistress would like to see him.

When he entered the room, Alexa rose to meet him.

"I thank you, Alexa, for your great kindness to Dawtie," he said. "Now perhaps I can better tell you what was on my heart two evenings ago."

He paused, looking for the right words. Finally he simply went ahead with the first ones that came to him.

"We were married in the prison. She is now my wife."

"Married—your wife!" echoed Alexa, flushing, and drawing a step back.

"I have loved her for years, and when she was in trouble, the time came for me to stand by her side."

"You had not spoken to her then—till—?"

"Not till last night. I said before the governor of the prison that I chose to take her for my wife. But if you please, we would like to have the proper ceremony as soon as possible."

"I wish I had known," said Alexa—almost to herself, with a troubled smile.

"I wish you had too," responded Andrew. "I am sorry to have made things difficult for you."

"You were doing nothing but being yourself, and have nothing to be sorry about."

Then she raised her face and looked into his with a look of confidence. "Will you please try to forget, Andrew?"

Nobility had carried the day. She had not one mean or selfish thought toward either him or the girl.

"To forget is not in a man's power, Alexa. But I shall never think a thought of you that you would wish unthought."

She held out her hand to him. They were friends forever.

"Will you be married here, Andrew? The house is at your service," she said.

"Don't you think it ought to be at her father's?"

"You are right," replied Alexa, and sat down.

Andrew stood in silence, for he saw she was meditating something. At length she raised her head and spoke.

"You took the step with Dawtie sooner than you intended, did you not?"

"Yes," answered Andrew.

"Then you can hardly be so well prepared as you might like to be."

"We shall manage."

"It will hardly be convenient for your mother, I fear. Your home is not large."

"No, but my mother loves us both, and where there has been room for me, there will now be room for her as well."

"Would you mind if I asked you how your parents took it?"

"They don't say much. I suppose we are all proud until we learn that we have one Master, and are all brethren. As your father no doubt looked down upon me, so do my father and mother tend to look down on Dawtie's family. But I have talked to them much, and they will soon get over it. We are all indeed one family, and God is not only our Father, he is our brother. If God was the mighty monarch so many represent him as, he would never have let us come near him."

"Did you hear Mr. Rackstraw's sermon on the condescension of God?" asked Alexa.

"The condescension of God! There is no such thing! How could God condescend to his children—their spirits born of his spirit, their hearts the children of his heart!"

His eyes flashed and his face shone. Alexa thought she had never seen him look so grand.

"I see," she answered. "I will never use the word about God again."

"Thank you," he said, then sighed deeply. "I am so tried by the things said about God," he went on, "by people who think they are pleasing him to speak so. I understand God's patience with the wicked, but I do wonder how he can be so patient with the pious!"

"They don't know better."

"They *would* know better if they wanted to! How are they to know better while they are so sure about everything? I would infinitely rather believe in no God at all than in such a God as they would have me believe in!"

Now it was Alexa's turn to sigh. She seemed thinking, and Andrew contented himself to wait until she was again ready to speak.

"Oh, Andrew," she finally said, "I used to not have a glimmer of what you meant when you spoke of God. Now I cannot even recall what it was I did not like in your teaching. I think it was that instead of listening and trying to grasp what you meant in your heart, I was always thinking of how I might oppose you with my mind. And I remember trying to find out what sect of belief you belonged to. I told people you did not believe this and did not believe that, when all the time I knew neither what you believed nor what you did not believe. I thought I did, but it was all mistake and imagination. I was so foolish and blind and conceited! When you would not discuss things with me, I thought you were afraid of losing the argument. Now I see that instead of disputing about opinions, I should have been saying, 'God be merciful to me a sinner!' "

"God be praised!" said Andrew. "You are a free woman at last, Alexa! The Father has called you, has been calling you all along, and now you have said, 'Here I am.' "

"I hope so, Andrew; thanks to God through you. I am so thankful to you for helping me at last to begin to see the true character of our Father!"

"We are all only beginning to see how wondrously *good* he is. His goodness is beyond what we can even imagine!"

"But I am forgetting what I wanted to say! Would it not be better—after you are married, I mean—to let Dawtie stay on with me a while? I will promise not to work her too hard," she added with a little laugh.

"It is just what I would expect of you! You want people to know that you believe in her after the incident with the cup."

"Yes. But I also want to do what I can for such good tenants as your two respective families. Therefore, I must add a room or two to your house, so that there will be good accommodations for you all. And perhaps there may be something I can do for Dawtie's parents as well!"

"You make thanks impossible! I will speak to Dawtie about it. I know she will be glad not to leave you. I will take care not to trouble you or the house by too much coming or going."

"Nonsense! You shall do just as you and Dawtie please.

Where Dawtie is, there will be room for you too. This will be just as much your home as it is mine for as long as you wish it!"

Already Alexa's pain had grown quite bearable in the outflow of her heart toward the two persons she loved more than she had ever loved in her life.

"Thank you! I think it best I remain with my parents for now. But I will accept your offer, and come freely and often."

Dawtie needed no persuading. She was so rich in the possession of Andrew that she could go an afternoon or a hundred years without seeing him, she said. The only change would be that he would not come to see her, but instead she would go to see him.

In ten days they were married at her father's cottage. Her father and mother accompanied her and Andrew to the Knowe, to dine with Andrew's father and mother. In the evening the new pair went out for a walk in the old fields.

"It seems that God's here, doesn't it, Dawtie?" said Andrew.

"Aye! But eh, it's like heaven itself to be out of that prison and walking about with you! God has given me all things!—just *all* things, Andrew!"

"God was with you in the prison, Dawtie."

"Aye! But I like better to be with him here!"

"And you may be sure he likes better to have you here!" rejoined Andrew.

32 / The Goblet Again

The next day Alexa and Dawtie set about searching the house yet again for the missing goblet. All the books in the study were removed and the place made utterly bare, but even the empty shelves gave no hint of concealment. They stood in its dreariness looking vaguely round them without so much as a clue.

"Did it ever come to you, ma'am," said Dawtie, "that a minute or two passed between Mr. Crawford coming down the stair with you, and me going back up to the master?"

"You are right, Dawtie, now that I think of it," replied Alexa.

"Well, when I went into the room, he lay panting in the bed. But as I brooded upon every piece of the thing when I was alone in prison, I found myself remembering that it seemed he had just come there a moment before me, in the bed I mean, as if he had climbed out of it and was just gotten into it again the same moment I came in. And what I'm thinking is—perhaps he got out to hide the cup."

"Dying people will do strange things!" rejoined her mistress. "You may well have solved half the mystery, Dawtie—why my father did not have it with him in the bed. But it brings us no nearer where the cup is at this moment."

"The surer we are it's here someplace, the better we'll seek," said Dawtie.

They began again and went over every inch of the room thoroughly, looking everywhere they could think of, even in the places they had been before. They had all but given it up to go on elsewhere when Dawtie, standing in the middle of the room and looking about in a sort of unconscious hopelessness, found her eyes resting on the mantelshelf. She walked over to it and laid her hand upon it. The mantel was of wood, and she fancied it a little loose, but she could not move it.

"When Andrew comes we'll get him to examine it," said Alexa.

He came in the evening, and Alexa told him what they had been doing. She asked him to get what tools he might need, and then to see whether there might be some space under the mantelshelf. But accustomed to thinking over the mechanical aspects of various contrivances with Sandy, Andrew wanted to have a closer look at it first. He presently came upon a clever little spring. When he pressed it he found he could lift the shelf. And there under it, sure enough, in rich response to the candle Alexa was holding behind him, flashed the gems of the curiously wrought chalice of gold!

Alexa gave a cry, Andrew drew a deep breath, and Dawtie laughed like a child.

Andrew carefully drew it out, and they passed it from one to the other, gazing on it, poring over the gems and the raised work that enclosed them. They then began to discuss among themselves what was to be done with it.

"We will send it to the earl," said Alexa.

"No," said Andrew; "that would be to make ourselves judges in the case. Your father must have paid money for it. Then he gave it to Mr. Crawford, and Mr. Crawford must not be robbed."

"Everything in the next room was left to my cousin," said Alexa, "along with the library of books only in this study. Whatever else was left him was individually described. The cup was not so listed, was not among the possessions in the next room, and is certainly not part of the library. Providence has left us to do with it as we may judge right. I think it ought to be taken to Borland Hall and restored to the heir of its rightful owner—and by Dawtie."

"And you will have her mention that your father bought it?"

"I will not take a shilling for it! I would not take the price of it even if my father had left the cup expressly to me. Nothing could make me touch money for it. George would never doubt we had concealed it in order to trick him out of it."

"He may think so all the same. It will convince him that Dawtie ought to have been convicted. In my interpretation of events, the thing is Mr. Crawford's, not yours. Your father undoubtedly meant him to have the cup, and God would not have you, even to serve the right, take advantage of an accident. Whatever ought to be done with the cup, Mr. Crawford ought to do it. It is his business to do right in regard to it, and whatever advantage may be gained by doing right, Mr. Crawford ought to have the chance of gaining it. Would you deprive him of the opportunity to which at least he has a right, of doing justice, and thus turning his soul toward the truth?"

"You would have us tell the earl that his cup is found but that Mr. Crawford claims it?" asked Alexa.

"We do not even know whether the earl knows of its existence. It is possible it has been out of his family for years and years."

"What Andrew would have us do, I think," supplemented Dawtie, "is take it to Mr. Crawford and tell him that the earl has a claim to it."

"Exactly!" rejoined Andrew. "My wife is already thinking like her husband! He should also be told where it was found, and because of that he has no *legal* right to it, nor any moral right to it than did the laird. Whereas we want to give him the opportunity of choosing to do right, we must also see that right is indeed done in the end. So after two weeks," continued Andrew, "if you find it is not in the earl's possession, I believe it would then be proper of you to tell George that you expect him to take it to the earl that he may buy it if he will, but that if George does not give him the opportunity, you will yourself go to the earl and apprise him of the situation and ascertain from him whether the offer has been made."

"That is just right!" said Alexa.

And so the thing was done. To his credit, George made the offer to Borland, and the cup is now in the earl's collection without the necessity of any further interference on Alexa's part.

A few days after she and Dawtie had taken the cup to Crawford, a parcel arrived at Potlurg. It contained a beautiful tiny silver box, and inside it the jewelled watch—with a letter from George, begging Alexa to accept his present, asking that, as they were cousins, might they not continue to be friends, and saying that the moment he annoyed her with any further petitions, she could return the watch. He expressed his regret that he had brought such suffering upon Dawtie, and said he was ready to make whatever amends her husband might think fit.

Andrew and George became, if not exactly friends, yet friendly neighbors. It is to be wondered whether George was capable of understanding Andrew's heart toward things. But to see them discussing a fine horse, or the state of the weather and local crops together, at least filled the mind with hope that the inward growth of the former had begun progressing in the right direction.

Alexa accepted the watch and wore it around her neck. She thought her father would like her to do so.

33 / The Hour Before Dawn

The friendship between Alexa, Dawtie, and Andrew was never broken. In adulthood it was as rich as had been the childhood bond between the latter two and Sandy. I will not say that, as she lay awake in the dark, the eyes of Alexa never renewed the tears of that autumn night on which she turned her back upon the pride of self. But her tears were never those of bitterness, self-scorn, or self-pity.

"If I am to be pitied," she would say to herself, "let the Lord pity me. I am not ashamed of what I did. And I have nothing to resent, for no one has wronged me."

Andrew died late in middle age. His wife said the Master wanted him for something nobody else could do, or he would not have taken him from her. She wept and took comfort, for she lived in expectation.

One night when she and Alexa were sitting together at Potlurg, about a month after his burial, speaking of many things with the freedom of a long and tested love and friendship, after a lengthy pause, Alexa said, "Were you not very angry with me then, Dawtie?"

"When?"

"When Andrew told you."

"Told me what? I can't think what you mean."

"When he told you I wanted him, not knowing he was yours."

"I know nothing of what you're talking about, Alexa," persisted Dawtie in a tone of bewilderment.

"Oh. I thought you had no secrets from each other."

"I don't know that we ever had—except things in his books that he said were God's secrets, which I would understand some-day, for God was telling them as fast as he could get his children to understand them."

"I see," sighed Alexa. "You were indeed made for each other!— But this is my secret, and I have the right to tell it. He kept it for me to tell you. I thought all the time you knew."

"I don't want to know anything Andrew would not tell me."

"He thought it was my secret, you see, not his, and that was why he did not tell you."

"Of course, I understand. Andrew always did what was right!"

"Well, then, Dawtie, I will tell you—I offered to be his wife if he would have me."

"And what did he say?" asked Dawtie, with the composure of one listening to a story learned from a book.

"He made me to understand that he couldn't. But I'm not sure what he *said*. The words went away."

"When was it you asked him?" said Dawtie, sunk in thought.

"Two nights before the trial," answered Alexa.

"He might have taken you, then, instead of me!—a lady and all! Oh, do you think he took me because I was in trouble? He might have been laird himself!"

"Dawtie! Dawtie!" cried Alexa. "You cannot possibly think my position weighed a straw with Andrew! If you think that, then I ought to have been his wife, for I know him better than you!"

Dawtie smiled at her words.

"But I do know," she said, "that Andrew was fit to cast the lairdship from him to comfort any poor lassie! I would have loved him all the same!"

"As I have done, Dawtie!" said Alexa solemnly. "But he wouldn't have thrown me away for you if he hadn't loved you, Dawtie. Be sure of that! He might have made nothing of the lairdship, but he wouldn't have made nothing of me! He loved all people too much for that."

"That's true, Alexa. I don't doubt it a moment."

"And I love him still—you mustn't mind me saying it, Dawtie. There are ways of loving that are good, though there be some pain in them. Thank God, we have our children to look after! You will let me say *our* children, won't you, Dawtie?"

In answer, Dawtie only smiled, the very smile that Andrew had always loved. And now it was Alexa's turn to cherish it as the smile of a true friend.

Some thought Alexa hard, some thought her cold. But the few that knew her knew she was neither. And some of my readers will grant that such a friend as Andrew was better than such a husband as George.